AUCTIONED TO THE ALPHA:
A TERRAMATES NOVEL

LISA LACE

CONTENTS

CHAPTER 1

"Hybrids, galaxy passport holders, and gentlemen of all species. Welcome to the Intergalactic Femme Matrona Exchange!"

As Thiago Arris swirled a golden liquid in his goblet, his ears perked up at the sound of the nasal voice behind him. He craned his neck towards the makeshift stage centered in the underground tavern. A single shaft of blue light illuminated the Mercurian standing at the podium.

The speaker was too small for the platform; his three-foot frame stood on a tower of stone slabs. The diminutive creature's row of beady, red eyes blinked sluggishly in turns. He had the bored expression of someone who spent innumerable hours working at a dead-end job. With his stumpy, trumpet-like ears twitching, his spindly fingers pressed down on the button of his choker, amplifying his voice across the seedy space.

"Please lower your ocular appendages to your screens and ensure your have preloaded your account with the 10,000 credit starting fee. The bidding will proceed in precisely five minutes."

The room of bidders had crowded into booths and segregated by choice into clusters of single species. Thiago's nose wrinkled in disgust. He counted about three dozen sleazy lowlifes assembled on the floor. They had traveled to this sleazy event from all corners of the Cassiopeia Galaxy. Most of the clients had a similar profile - wealthy older alien males looking for a good time.

Grunts of approval rumbled around the room. A few men fidgeted with the translation devices strapped around their ears. They were obvious first-timers, here to pop their bidding cherry. The ones that sat slumped in their seats with hands hovering over their screens, gazes narrowed and minds ready to bid....those were the clear veterans.

In the front of the room, Thiago recognized Admiral Izra. The Noxx were one of the most feared species in the galaxy. Izra was a high-ranking official with an incurable gambling addiction and a penchant for squandering his dirty money at intergalactic brothels. Though several other intimidating parties surrounded the mighty creature, including a table of twelve-foot grumpy Gigan businesspeople with their heads awkwardly tilted against the ceiling, he stood out like a hungover soldier reporting for duty.

With his pierced snout, a gnarled crown of feathers surrounding his head, and slippery, ghost-white scales covering his entire body, he was an impossible sight to overlook. Coupled with the retractable webbed wings of the Noxx, Izra looked like an evolutionary mistake.

"Please refrain from resting your tentacles against the cushions. Bodily slime is a nasty stain difficult to remove!" the auctioneer yelled, glaring at a group of Thesbians in the back row. Turning to the curtains behind him, he called out to an unseen subordinate. "Maliah. Bring out the items from Batch 799!"

A stout Mercurian hobbled out from behind the curtains, dragging a line of nude women shackled together in heavy iron chains. In single file, they stumbled onto the stage behind him, sickly and shivering. Thiago winced, finding it almost unbearable to look at them. But he kept his face a stoic slate.

He didn't flinch as bidders erupted in chaotic slurs around him, catcalling and propositioning the women in their native languages. Deep scrapes and infected gashes adorned their joints and limbs from nonstop hard labor. The women appeared resigned to their fates, blinking at the boisterous crowd with glazed, unfocused eyes.

"First, we have number 28749," the auctioneer announced, slamming his fist down and pushing a button on the control pad of the podium.

The woman on the far left yelped in pain. She jumped when the collar around her neck started to emit sparks. Her scraggly, dishwater-blonde hair shielded her face as she rubbed helplessly at her throat. The woman didn't look up; her deadened eyes stared at the ground. Metallic sounds echoed around the room as creatures pounded on their screens. The prices were accelerating at an alarming rate.

"43,000 credits is currently the highest bid," the auctioneer declared rapidly, retrieving a set of spectacles that accommodated all his eyes. "44,000 – going once, going twice...*sold* to the gentleman in Booth 14."

The bidders in Booth 14 broke out in celebratory whoops; the rest of the crowd moaned in disgust. A pair of Noxx guards ushered the blonde woman down the steps towards her new husband, a southern Vishyan flaunting flashy jewelry and thick patches of chest hair. The gravity of her situation finally registered in her mind. She shook with fear. With a wobbling bottom lip, she sandwiched herself between the blue-fleshed, four-armed creatures.

One by one, the women onstage were swiftly auctioned off. When every woman in the first group had a buyer, the auctioneer introduced the Special Collection. The only thing special about the collection was the price. The opening bid was a hefty 750,000 credits. A large screen descended from behind him, stopping short of the floor. A projector opposite the room noisily crackled as it turned on and displayed the profiles of the new imports.

Files were transferred containing physical descriptions and photographs of Earth women from different countries. The Company treated the Special Collection women differently. Their pictures showed carefully arranged hairstyles and beautiful faces painted with make-up. They appeared cheerful, blissfully unaware of their impending fates.

Thiago swigged down the rest of his lunar brandy and slid his empty goblet back to the bartender, paying for his drink. He made it halfway toward the back exit when he caught sight of one of the women on someone else's computer. He stopped abruptly, clutching a throbbing mark on his forehead.

He had to have her.

He turned back toward the bidding pit. He paused, studying the woman shown on the screen. She had untamed, coppery-red hair and vivid green eyes. Her pouting lips were slightly parted. Thiago cracked his knuckles and pulled the hood of his cloak over his head, concealing his features in the shadows. Grumbling under his breath, he moved undetected into an empty booth in the back row.

Izra would be the only competition for his mate. The creature bared a set of gritted, jagged teeth as he tapped on his screen intently. Logging in, Thiago pressed the bid button on his screen. He watched with a satisfied smirk as Izra's wings flapped out in rage, knocking his goons onto the floor on either side of him. Izra whirled around, snarling furiously with a maddened look in his eyes as he tried to figure out who was bidding against him. Thiago used Izra's distraction to his advantage, finalizing the bid on the girl.

"950,000...no...one *million* credits going once, going twice...*sold* to the gentleman in Booth 33. Congratulations, sir! We will deliver your bride in three to five business days."

Izra sprang up from his seat, a deafening roar erupting from his throat and rocking the tavern. He moved around wildly in a blind rage, causing dust and rock particles from the roof to come down on the other bidders. His eyes narrowed to threatening slits as he looked at Booth 33. It was empty now, but he caught a glimpse of a figure slipping through the swinging back exit. His hands curled into fists, plowing into an innocent bystander.

CHAPTER 2

24 HOURS EARLIER

"You know this isn't fair, Peter."

Eden's middle-aged employer fingered the edges of his grease-spattered apron. Staring uneasily at the grimy floors of the kitchen, he purposely avoided looking in the eyes of his employee. Her back-and-forth pacing was beginning to make him a little queasy. Scratching at the back of his neck and flicking away the guilty sweat trickling down, he tried to reason with her.

"Eden, I'm sorry, but my decision's final," he began. His bushy mustache wiggled under his bulbous nose as he sniffed. "I gave you a couple of chances after you came in late a few times. You acted up the other night. We can't afford to have you scaring away any more of our customers."

"Acting up? I don't care how regular of a client Mr. Paisley is. That creep grabbed a handful of my left tit! All I did was defend myself and knock him on his ass. I could have done a lot worse. Besides, someone got it on camera. The video's going viral. If anything, I'm bringing you publicity and deserve a bonus."

To make her point, the woman yanked open the door to the dining area. Jabbing a finger at the bustling atmosphere of the fully-occupied diner, she finished bitterly, "I would appreciate it if you didn't give me any of your crap."

"Don't start with me, Eden. You're a good waitress, but you're too tense. You need to learn how to go with the flow a little more. I'm sure you'll find something else soon enough."

"That was textbook sexual harassment! You know what? I could sue you for this," she blurted. Her face instantly blushed when she saw the smug expression on her employer's face.

It was an unspoken understanding. Both knew perfectly well it was an empty threat. She wasn't about to take anyone to court over a waitress job that barely dished out the state of New York's minimum wage. She swallowed her smart remarks, doing her best to ignore the shaking heads of the line cooks.

They had their backs turned away from her. They pretended not to listen and continued their duties amidst the drama. Hanging her head in defeat, she marched towards the employee lockers and began to empty out her belongings. She pulled on an old jacket and slid her purse onto her shoulder, stomping towards the exit.

"Eden, wait."

"Yes?"

She spun around, her round eyes glimmering with hope.

"Do you want to bring home one of the cornbread muffins you like so much? This one's on the house, free of charge."

Fuming, she rolled her eyes and stormed out the rear door of the diner.

"You know what, Peter, you keep that muffin to yourself. Do me a favor and shove it up your ass."

The door slammed shut in her face, inches from her nose.

"Your muffin was dry and bland as hell!" she barked at the closed door. "I've had better!"

As Eden held her jacket close to her body, a cloud of fluffy stuffing wheezed out from the parka. She trudged across the slushy snow coating the sidewalks of Bedford Avenue. It was taking everything in her to stay stable. The struggle to stay warm was the only thing preventing her from shattering. Crying wouldn't have made her feel better. The gusty winds of the harsh Brooklyn winter would have frozen her tears solid.

Eden stopped in front of an elderly vendor with a toothy smile. The fragrant steam wafting from his cart grabbed her attention. She decided to treat herself to a falafel pita sandwich and plopped down on a ledge across the mobile eatery. Her mouth was watering, and she greedily bit into her food. The sandwich was too hot, and she finally lost control. Eden's eyes welled up with tears. The flavor of the Middle Eastern dish was lost on her scorched taste buds as she angrily threw the meal away from her.

"Great," she muttered sarcastically, scowling at her sandwich. She had scattered it across the pavement.

"Is it okay if I sit here?"

Eden inched aside, smiling weakly at a dark-haired woman rolling up next to her, pushing a grocery cart filled with junk.

"Of course."

The stranger raked a hand through her brusquely chopped pixie cut as she settled next to Eden. She stuffed a hand into the pocket of her flimsy windbreaker, producing a half-crushed box of Newports. Slipping a cigarette between her chapped lips, she offered one to Eden.

"Want one? Don't take this the wrong way, but you look like you had a rough day."

Eden hadn't smoked since high school, and even then, she only blackened her young lungs to fit in with the cool kids. But with her life going to hell at this point, she desperately needed a vice to keep her head from imploding. Shrugging, she gladly accepted a cigarette, allowing the stranger to light up for her.

"Thanks. Are you hungry?"

"Always. Anything helps."

Eden handed her a crumpled five-dollar bill as a slight wave of smoke drifted out of her lips.

"Thanks, I appreciate that. You know, if you need to vent or anything, I'm all ears."

"Um, that's all right."

"You don't have to be uncomfortable about my situation. We've all got problems. Let me guess. It's around two in the afternoon now, and you're cruising the streets with a bunch of your stuff. Did you just get canned?"

"You must be a detective," Eden quipped, nodding. "I won't miss getting boils on my arms from the deep fryer or scrubbing vomit off the countertops. It was a shitty job, but it paid money."

"I understand. I worked in telemarketing for a while, but I was let go. Long story short, I lived paycheck to paycheck and student loans were killing me. Next thing you know, here I am."

"That's tough."

"Wait a second. I *know* you. You're that girl from that video, aren't you? One of my friends showed it to me when I crashed at his place yesterday. You made the front page of World Star. With good reason – that dude sailed! Where'd you learn to fight like that?"

"The martial arts club I joined back in high school paid off, I guess. I took some free self-defense classes at Hard Knocks Gym down at 5th too," said Eden pointedly, crushing the cigarette stub under her sneakers. "It ended up with me getting fired. I keep waiting to feel some remorse, but I don't. You know what? If I could rewind time to that day, I'd do the same thing. The only difference is, this time, we'd both get locked up."

"That's why you got fired?" the stranger asked, tutting disapprovingly. "That's low. I'm sorry, you want another cig?"

"No, I'm good, thanks," Eden declined, her shoulders sagging. "It wouldn't be so bad if I were on my own. You know me. Well, I guess you don't, but I'm the queen of bouncing back. It's tough this time, though. Dad's cancer has spread to his stomach. His medical bills are piling up. My sister Janine's tuition fees are due in two weeks."

The stranger listened to her quietly, inserting appropriate "mms" and "ahs" at the correct moments as Eden unloaded her thoughts.

"I moonlight as a cleaner at a department store. I babysit for one of my neighbors too, but that's just on Tuesdays and weekends. The job at the diner was our main bread and butter."

"Do you ever sleep? I wouldn't want to be in your shoes, either. I wish there were something I could do to help you, but I've only got good vibes to spread around."

"Thanks for listening. I feel a little better, I suppose," mumbled Eden, exhaling glumly. She reached into her purse for her thermos and began wrestling with the busted lid. "It's just been...ah, crap."

She'd yanked a little too hard. Coffee spurted out of her thermos, spraying onto her clothes. The stranger frowned and began rummaging through her cart. She handed Eden a crumpled flier to mop up the coffee bleeding onto her jeans.

"I think I pissed off a god of fortune today or something."

Eden flattened the flier between her fingertips, but just as she began sweeping it against her damp thigh, something caught her eye. As she reread the obscure wording on the flier, a single, inquisitive eyebrow began rising.

"Where'd you get this? Can I keep it?"

"Sure. A man was handing them out at Empire Boulevard." The stranger snorted. "I'm pretty sure that thing's a..."

"Hey, thanks for everything. I have to go now. Take care!"

"...scam." By the time the stranger completed her sentence, Eden had already disappeared around the corner.

Eden hopped off the bus and looked thoughtfully at a flier she must have read over a hundred times. She walked toward a narrow, four-story building wedged between two lofty skyscrapers. With all the upscale boutiques and modern office towers lining Hawthorne Road, the building appeared strikingly ordinary. An old, hand-painted sign bore a single word in faded crimson — TerraMates.

Eden supposed they were going for function over style. As she crept closer to the building and peeked through the sealed blinds of a window, beads of perspiration collected on her forehead.

Part of her wanted to turn around and walk back to the bus stop without even going into the building. Another part that dominated her thinking urged her to stay. It wasn't like she was born yesterday. In this part of town, matchmaking was nothing like reality television.

Candidates weren't paired up based on mutual hobbies and interests. You were filed into separate categories based on your physical description, the size of your chest, and you were shipped off to the highest bidder. Her head spun thinking about the danger.

At the same time, an image of her father appeared in her mind's eye. They had said their goodbyes before she left for work that morning.

Cancer had reduced his sturdy build to a sad, bedridden shadow of himself. Sallow skin clung to his bones, and the countless rounds of chemotherapy had him struggling to keep his eyes open for more than an hour or two at a time. These were the remnants of a man who had put his professional quarterback aspirations on hold to raise two young girls abandoned by their mother.

And of course, there was Janine – an absolute genius blessed with street smarts and academic intelligence. When Eden was unable to complete community college because their father fell ill, the goal-driven Janine was the only person in the family who stood a chance to escape their family's cycle of poverty.

In the end, Eden was already in front of TerraMates, and she had nowhere else to be at the moment. Perhaps today she would be pleasantly surprised. Was a cultured European gentleman who had lost his wife and was looking for companionship waiting for her? Ignoring the tight knots lacing her stomach, she gently pushed open the front door to the building.

Eden tried not to gawk at her surroundings, but she could feel her chin slowly lowering in amazement. Inside the building was a spotless office with state-of-the-art equipment and floors so white you could check your teeth for lipstick smears off of it. TerraMates agents attended to attractive young women inside straight rows of cubicles.

She hesitated and nervously fiddled with the worn strap of her purse. As she lost her nerve and turned her body back toward the entrance, a woman in a sleek, all-black pantsuit and a bleached, shoulder-length bob caught up to her. She smiled and stretched her arms over the door, barring the exit.

"Welcome to TerraMates. Are you lost?"

"Sorry," said Eden hurriedly. "It looks like you're full. I'll come back another time."

"Nonsense, I'll take care of you personally," said the woman cheerfully, the bangles on her arms jingling as she beckoned her forward. "I'm Jennifer Daley, the director here. Please, follow me."

Eden's forehead wrinkled warily as her eyes drifted back to the door handle. Sucking air in through her teeth, she moved her stubborn feet and followed Ms. Daley to a tubular, glass elevator at the far end of the office. They arrived on the basement floor. Eden watched as they walked past a display of flashing lights behind curtains, ending up at what appeared to be photo booth stations.

"What's your name?"

"Eden. Eden Castle."

"Great, Eden. You're beautiful, by the way. Frank will hold your things for you," Ms. Daley ordered, taking Eden's belongings and shoving them to a skinny man wearing an ill-fitting doctor's coat. "First things first. Let's have your picture taken. "

"My picture?" Eden repeated, puzzled. Ms. Daley pulled her behind a curtain and placed her on a seat in front of a white backdrop. Eden brushed a finger across her lips self-consciously and grabbed a handful of her unruly, unwashed hair. "I'm not exactly presentable right now."

It was too late. She heard a camera take a few pictures, and she blinked furiously. She saw spots from the sudden flash of light.

"That will do. Follow me, please."

Eden shook her head, feeling naked without any of the possessions she had brought into the establishment. This was already one of the strangest interviews she had experienced, and this included a prospective employer from Brooklyn Heights, who would only address her breasts. Still, against her better judgment, Eden followed behind Ms. Daley, who was walking to her private office in stiletto heels.

"Please, have a seat."

Eden pulled up a chair opposite to Ms. Daley. Her hands rested uncomfortably on her lap as she looked at a woman whose features were rendered indecipherable from years of botox treatments. Frank entered the room a few moments later, handing the director a clipboard and a thick manila folder. As Frank retired silently to the corner, Ms. Daley skimmed through the contents of the clipboard before finally breaking the silence.

"Can I get you anything to drink?"

"No, thank you."

"Eden, I take it this is your first time interacting with the matchmaking industry."

"Is it that obvious?" said Eden. She noticed she was jiggling her leg self-consciously and tried to stop it. "I'm not sure how this works, exactly. To be honest, I need the money."

"It looks like you're in luck. How would you feel about being stationed...overseas? There is a gentleman who's willing to pay quite a bit for a natural redhead."

Goose bumps appeared on Eden's covered arms as she listened to the nonchalant objectification coming from the woman's lips. Ms. Daley made it sound like she was offering Eden bonus health and security benefits. Eden opened her mouth to speak, but Ms. Daley, perhaps sensing her reluctance, spoke again.

"I apologize for the bluntness. Sometimes I forget it's everyone else's first time. Here," said Ms. Daley, pulling out a massive contract from a folder and sliding it across the table. "Our agency guarantees your safety and well-being, as well as a complete confidentiality clause."

Ms. Daley's words dwindled to static in Eden's ears as her eyes focused on the total amount in bold, sitting front and center on the first page of the agreement.

"Is this a typo? All these credits up front?" Eden asked in disbelief.

It couldn't be real. With all this money, they'd be able to fly her father to Dallas for the treatment he desperately needed. They could start paying the mortgage on the house again. Janine's tuition bills would be paid. Even better, they would be able to afford a school she deserved. This was too sweet of a treat, and up until this point in her life, they had not existed.

"The contract is real," said Ms. Daley. "That's why I was so forward with you in the first place. If you're not interested, there are plenty of others waiting in line behind you."

Where am I going?, Eden thought to herself. What she said was, "Where do I sign"? She grabbed the fountain pen resting on the table.

Ms. Daley leaned forward eagerly, flipping over page after page as Eden hastily scribbled her signature in circles and across dotted lines. But as Eden was busily signing her initials on the last page, she failed to notice Frank's figure sneaking up behind her.

As soon as Eden lifted the point of the pen off the crisp sheet, she smelled the peculiar scent of rubber and latex. She thrashed her arms but stopped struggling when she felt a sharp prick on the side of her neck.

Within seconds, Eden had slumped over the chair.

CHAPTER 3

AFTER THE AUCTION

Drip. Drip. Drip.

Eden stirred, blindly batting at the dripping liquid. The leaky roof was on her to-do list to repair, but she had not gotten around to it yet. Groggily, she lifted her aching arms to wipe the rain water from her cheeks.

As her fingertips touched the cold, slimy liquid, her face scrunched up like she had accidentally tasted a sour lemon. She wiped away the slobber with her sleeves and slowly sat up. As soon as her eyes snapped open, a scream erupted out of her dry throat.

"Oh my goodness," Eden choked, scurrying backward and bracing herself against a wall.

A creature the size of a miniature horse stood in front of her. It wasn't an animal you could find at a zoo, and it certainly wasn't one you wanted making its nest in your closet. The horrifying hybrid had eight amber eyes set around giant, beetle-like pincers, with eight hairy legs to match. Its claws clicked noisily in excitement as it crawled forward, tilting its head as if it was sizing her up. She poked at her face and ears with slippery hands, crying out in pain. The pink pinch marks from the animal hurt when she touched them.

Eden covered her face, hoping her hands would provide sufficient protection against impending doom. "No!

Please go away!" Eden gasped, kicking her legs randomly as she peeked through the gaps in her fingers. "I know we've got sewer rats the size of dogs in New York, but this is ridiculous. Leave me alone! Help! Janine?"

"Hercules, heel!"

The Arachtera backed off and sat on the ground using its opposable legs. A tall man stepped forward, his face obscured by a thick hood draped over his head. He wore a leather-brown outfit. In the haunting green lights of the room, his silhouette was bathed in a seductive glow. Eden's grip loosened around the tangle of hair she held in a death grip.

She stared in awe at the figure's one-piece suit. It was certainly handmade and fitted with multiple pockets, trinkets, and small gadgets she'd never come across before. She was hopeless with technology but liked watching other people use it.

"Thanks for that. I didn't know what I was going to do," said Eden. She dusted herself off as she rose to her feet. She froze as she got a better look at her surroundings. Her knees wobbled beneath her and threatened to dump her on the ground again. "Wait a second. Where am I?"

"What's your name?"

The deep, beautiful tone of his voice rattled her, but she wouldn't give up. "Don't answer my question with another question. I'm serious!"

"What is your name?"

"I...Eden. Look, sir, whatever this is, I need to get back home."

"Don't call me sir," the man interjected firmly. "My name is Thiago Arris."

"Okay, Mr. Arris. Did you make that name up yourself? Or is it Greek or something?" said Eden. She nodded to herself slowly, crossing her arms as if she'd figured everything out.

"I'm not really in the mood for any of this. I just had a hell of a dream. Janine put you up to it, didn't she? This elaborate prank is exactly the kind of joke my sister enjoys. It's just like her to try and hit me months before April, too, so she can catch me off-guard."

"I do not know who Janine is."

"Yeah, okay," Eden sang, fixing her arms on her hips mockingly. "Let me guess, it's Jeffrey under the hood using a voice modulator."

She strode towards Hercules, slanting her head to the side to study the creature. She was impressed. Her bottom lip stuck out as she remarked, "And that, of course, would be Caleb. Where did you guys get this suit? These costumes must have cost you all a fortune. I have got to hand it to you, though. It is extremely lifelike. You almost got me. Almost. Hey, Caleb, think fast!"

Eden reached into the pocket of her parka, fishing for a brown, half-eaten apple in a clear bag. She hurled it at the creature, expecting it to bounce off its head. Instead of watching an annoyed teenager burst out of a costume, Hercules leaped in mid-air and caught the apple with its pincers. An unmistakably real mouth opened to reveal circular rows of yellow teeth gobbling up the juicy fruit.

She leaped back once again and screeched. She wasn't going to be unarmed this time. Eden snatched a thick, glassy rod from the table next to her and wielded it like a sword.

"Unless you intend on performing Herc's annual health exam, you should put it down. You're holding his rectal thermometer."

Eden dropped the thermometer immediately. Mortified, she began rubbing her hands raw against her jeans. The air filled with rapid-fire cursing.

"Calm down," said Thiago, laughing. "He's more afraid of you than you are of him."

"That sounds nice, but I don't think that applies to Satan's spawn."

Eden looked around for a place to wash her hands. A living room, kitchen, and a workshop area were all crowded onto the first floor of the loft-like space. A short, spiraling staircase led up to a dark room littered with clothing and an unmade mattress. Sunlight streamed into the first floor through multiple windows. She ground her teeth together and braced herself as she dashed towards the closed circular windows embedded in the dense, pale walls. Inserting her finger into an opening at the center, she began to pry it open with all her strength.

"Hey, what are you doing? You don't want to open those!"

"Why don't you have regular windows like a normal person?" Eden angrily muttered as she pulled back in a huff. "What do you do for air around here?" She ran her fingers through her hair and over her neck, accidentally brushing the small puncture wound.

"Ow! No way. This can't be happening, can it? Did those people at TerraMates drug me? I knew Ms. Daley was a little odd. I haven't said goodbye to my family, I haven't packed...none of this makes sense. Is this legal? It's kidnapping!" She rambled on, answering her questions as a nonplussed Thiago stared blankly at her.

Behind Thiago, Hercules whimpered sympathetically. The creature attempted to approach her but retreated into position with one reproachful look from his master. As Thiago stared at Eden, whose frantic speech was rising in pitch every second, he wasn't sure what his next move should be. His knowledge of proper Earth etiquette was a little rusty. The last time he'd interacted with one was over a decade ago.

Clearing his throat, he lifted his arm to signal it was now his turn to speak, but his motion only aggravated her.

"Don't you dare point your finger at me. I demand you tell me where we are, right now!"

"We're on planet HT-007. Please, if you could keep your voice down and your emotions in check, it would make everything a lot easier to explain."

"Excuse me? Planet what, now?" Eden asked incredulously. She buried her head in her arms in confusion. "I can't even see you. Would you please take that damn hood off? Look, I'm sorry, Mr. Arris...."

"My name is Thiago."

"Thiago," Eden repeated through clenched teeth. "There's been a misunderstanding. I need you to hand over my purse so I can call and arrange for some way out of here. Are we still in North America? Central America, maybe? China?"

"You arrived with no possessions. I could check, but I don't think you can call home. It's a long way away," Thiago stonily replied as he leaned back against the wall.

"Now you're on a budget? I'll reimburse you for the long distance fees. Give me my things or I'm going to be forced to call the cops on you."

"The what?"

"The cops! The po-po? The fuzz?" said Eden loudly as she tried to latch her zipper onto the other end of her parka. "The guys that are going to come and handcuff your sorry ass, charging you and everyone else at TerraMates with twenty to life for kidnapping. Oh, forget it."

Eden was flustered and dropped her head into her hands. She wandered aimlessly around Thiago's spaceship. Eden wasn't sure what she wanted to find. One thing was certain – she wouldn't be going anywhere with him. She stomped down on a glowing green pedal on the floor of the wall adjacent to her. The wall split open, granting her access to the cockpit.

"Hey, wait a minute! Don't go anywhere!"

Eden had time for one brief glance at the controls before a wayward breeze brushed her cheek. She realized the door to the cockpit was slightly cracked open. Eden jumped on the opportunity and forcefully opened the door. Casting one final glimpse at Thiago behind her, she slipped out the door and sprinted into the darkness. The sound of his voice faded behind her.

CHAPTER 4

Eden stopped running. She gasped for breath as she looked back at Thiago's spaceship, which was now about the size of a coin. As Eden clamped a hand over her heavily thumping heart, she twirled around in place. What was she going to do now? She was in the middle of nowhere without any indication of civilization around her.

"I wonder if they sent me off to live with a serial killer," Eden thought out loud.

Her heart sank. Without warning, her cheeks ballooned with vomit. She turned to her side and hurled her upset stomach's contents onto the ground. Her chest still heaved, but her head felt refreshingly lighter as she shuffled away from the crime scene.

Wherever she was, it wasn't wintertime here. Eden was overheating in her Brooklyn winter attire. She stripped down to a white tank top, tying her parka and flannel shirt around her waist. Eden started down a path, decided to head straight for the horizon to find some help. Eden paced herself, knowing she had wasted energy with the adrenaline rush that had gotten her all the way here.

Her sneakers slapping against the gravel on the ground sounded like a lonely poltergeist walking back and forth in an abandoned attic. She was a nervous wreck and believed she had escaped from a murderer. Her teeth chattered despite the muggy heat of the windless terrain as her mind flooded with worst-case-scenarios, most of them ending with her body detached from her head and buried in a shallow grave. She felt a heavy sense of regret. She scolded herself for not trusting the peculiar feeling that she felt before stepping foot into TerraMates.

Snapping out of her self-pity, she slowed to a stop and frowned. She squinted her eyes up at the night sky covered with a thin haze of golden fog. The moon peeked out of a cluster of clouds and helped to illuminate her path. As she squatted to examine the ground, she quickly realized something was different here, and she hadn't stumbled onto a strange eclipse changing the color of her surroundings.

Eden scooped a mound of dirt into her hands. Its texture was like grains of sand as it cascaded through the spaces between her fingers. It had a dark, almost violet hue to it. The landscape surrounding her looked like it had popped out of a Halloween cartoon. Bright orange plants resembling cacti dotted the horizon. A handful of ten-foot leafless trees with purple bark spread around the vast stretch of land.

She sprang up from the ground and rubbed the dirt off her hands. Other than her daring escape from her crazy hermit "husband" who'd undoubtedly bred and nurtured the monstrosity he called a pet, she felt astonishingly well-rested. Had TerraMates injected her with a sedative that contained hallucinogens? Perhaps this sad wasteland was a toxic dump site created to give government conspiracy theorists something to discuss. As she looked on at the flora, watching as they appeared to move around without a breeze displacing them, she decided it was probably the former.

"Alright, Eden. You've got this," she said, her voice slicing through the icy stillness. The sound of her voice calmed her jumpy heartbeat. "You've never needed anyone to look out for you before. Now it's finally time to look out for yourself. You knocked a full-grown man onto his ass for disrespecting you a few days ago, and he was twice your size. You've got..."

Eden's self-coaching trailed off. Her widening eyes spied two, tepee-style tents in front of her. Sighing in relief, she scampered forward. As she approached the neglected site, however, the grin on her face swiftly faded.

Gathering her unmanageable curls over on one side of her neck, she stepped with slow, calculated footsteps. A blackened pile of burnt firewood sat between the tents, accompanied by copper pots, stained sheets, and something unidentifiable. Her budding curiosity got the better of her. Eden picked up a twig on the ground and stuck it under the filmy, mottled matter.

It was skin.

"Well, this is gross."

The semitransparent skin looked reptilian. Although science was never one of her best subjects, she was confident in asserting one particular fact. Whatever had shed the skin was enormous. She shook her head, tossing the twig to the corner. As with every clue that came her way, she was growing increasingly dumbfounded about her whereabouts.

31

What was more, she was usually an annoyingly light sleeper. She woke up multiple times every night to her sister Janine's tossing and turning. It still boggled her mind how she was able to sleep through the plane ride, boat voyage, or however they smuggled her to this godforsaken place.

"Okay, snap out of it," Eden reminded herself, consciously clearing her mind of all the questions pecking away at her.

She dropped to her knees and rifled through the tents, hoping to find a forgotten cell phone or tablet left behind by the drifters. Instead, she uncovered bags of trinkets and devices she'd never seen before, as well as more shed skin tucked away beneath the sheets. Her mouth dropped open, the worst of possibilities beginning to run through her mind. What if the drifters hadn't left the site, and a dangerous animal ate them? What if that thing decided to revisit the campsite?

Panicking, she quickly crawled out of the tent, coming face to boots with two thin, lanky men in oversized vests and fitted leggings. The shadows cast by one of the leafless trees behind them hid their faces. Overwhelmed with gratitude for any company, she quickly bounced up to her feet.

"Hey guys, I'm sorry to intrude," she said, raising her hands cautiously. "I wasn't trying to steal anything. I seem to be lost. Could you help a girl out?"

The men lowered their heads. They appeared to be listening to her but chose to remain silent.

"I know this is going to sound crazy, but could you tell me where we are? Do you even speak English?"

Eden was desperate, and she wasn't going to give up. She stepped forward and pretended she was using a phone. "Can I borrow one of your phones?"

Their features became distinct the closer she approached. To a distant eye, the men could pass for another pair of broke, slightly underfed transients drifting from city to city. A careful observer would realize they were not transients. Along with their greasy, grayish mops of hair, the cracked flesh of the humanoid creatures was sickly white. They looked like dropped porcelain dolls hastily glued back together. A marking of a red "U" intersected with two arrows facing up was on each of their foreheads.

"Sorry," Eden squeaked, edging away from them. "I'll just be on my way now. Please don't kill me."

They lunged at her. Eden managed to throw out her leg and hook onto one of their ankles, sweeping one of the attackers off of his feet. Attacking the one made her vulnerable to the other, who was now looking at her back. The one on his feet leered, snaking his hands under Eden's arms and hauling her to the ground. Rubbing his head, the fallen drifter regained his balance, wrapping her flailing legs in a tight, unbreakable grip.

"*Let go of me!*"

Eden's screams rang into the night, making the pulsating beat in her ears go into overdrive. Out of nowhere, a vicious hissing sounded next to her. The velvet bristles of Hercules' legs wrapped around each of her attackers. Stunned, the two instantly released Eden to deal with the new threat, dropping her carelessly onto the ground. Hercules' rock-solid grip had trapped the aliens. The growling Arachtera flung the men to the side and catapulted them high into the air.

"Hercules, good boy!" Eden gushed, stroking the creature's head as he nuzzled against her, cooing appreciatively.

"Is there a problem here?"

Thiago stalked towards her. As he bent forward, offering his hand, his hood fell onto his shoulders. Eden's pupils swelled. The knots in her chest unraveled as she gazed intensely at him. He was clean-shaven and appeared to be in his mid-thirties, with unusual patterns shaved into his bed of pale, platinum-blonde hair. She found it especially difficult to tear away from the surreal, steely blue stare of his eyes.

Two golden hoops on Thiago's cocked left eyebrow wiggled as he waved his hand in front of her face.

"Are you going take my hand or not?"

"Sorry," Eden muttered, grabbing his hand. She glanced up at Thiago fleetingly, who stood a head taller than her. She noticed a similar flesh-toned marking on his forehead as on her attackers. Thiago's mark was subtle. "What were those things?"

"Arkadians," Thiago replied curtly. Apparently he thought that would answer her question.

"Huh? Never mind. But listen. Thanks for coming after me. I guess we got off on the wrong foot."

"I told you to stay. You should have listened to me," said Thiago unpleasantly, strutting off in the opposite direction. "*Humans.*"

"Don't give me the side-eye," Eden called after him, jogging to stay alongside Thiago as Hercules skipped next to the heated pair. "Could you blame me? I still have no idea where I am."

"Are all of you like this?"

"All of us? You mean, women?" Eden yelled, unable to contain herself. "What are we like exactly?"

"No. Humans. Are you all this ungrateful?"

"Wow," said Eden, clapping her hands dryly. "That's rich coming from someone who took an abducted victim."

"You know what?"

"No, I don't know what."

Thiago reached into his cloak and pulled out a device, whispering a few words into it. Eden's words cut short as the ground vibrated underneath them. Thiago's spaceship maneuvered to them on auto-pilot. As wind came from the engine, blowing the hair out of Eden's face, not a single sound escaped her mouth. The ship made a shaky

35

landing as it lowered itself to the ground, landing a few feet away from them.

"I *saved* you." Thiago shook his head. "Why don't I just show you?"

Petrified but intrigued, Eden followed him, tentatively boarding the spaceship.

Thiago set coordinates for the nearest city. Eden sat shotgun next to Thiago as Hercules entertained himself in the back with his scratching post. She appeared tense. Her back was rigidly placed an inch away from the triangular end of her chair. Her fingers unconsciously drummed along her thighs.

"What are we doing?"

"I'm proving my point," Thiago replied. He reached over his control panel to lower the shields on the window from the passenger's side. "Go ahead. Look for yourself."

"No way," Eden whispered. Her breath fogged up the glass as she peered through the window. "This can't be real."

Thiago steered the spaceship with double-pronged controls, smoothly coasting past buildings and infrastructure set on multiple levels of the city. Eden was amazed to see robust, circular tubes crisscrossing elevated pods like interlinking elevators. She gasped, pointing her finger at a group of blue-skinned creatures in formal suits moving up a pipe, separating at an intersection and disembarking into different pods. Spotting a family of big creatures with chubby, humanoid torsos and six tentacles, she squealed.

"What did I tell you?" asked Thiago softly, clicking his tongue as he looked out his side of the window.

"They're adorable!"

Thiago followed her line of vision and shook his head. "No, not those weirdos." The craft jerked sideways, flying over an exceptionally busy pod that featured tall casino towers and gambling stations. He pulled down a lever to enlarge the view through their primary window. Thiago leaned back in his seat as he folded his arms across his chest.

"Those weirdos."

As she watched, Eden could feel the blood in her veins grow cold. Creatures wearing expensive clothing and glittering jewels swarmed in and out of the pod. Although dolled-up alien partners accompanied a few, most were dragging scantily-clad human women with leashes hooked onto their shock collars. The women seemed well-fed and had faces donned with glittery, colorful make-up and hair pulled back in elaborate up-dos, but misery was written all over their vapid expressions.

"To my knowledge, there's no return trip to Earth. Have you finally gotten it through that thick human skull of yours?"

Thiago paused, his face softening abruptly as his eyes rested on the passenger next to him. Her head was hung low. Her large, mossy-green eyes glistened as they welled with tears. Deliberately blinking to keep them from falling, she turned away from the alien. She chose instead to look out her side of the window with her chin cupped in her hands.

Thiago cringed, feeling a sharp pulse on his forehead. The self-righteous, superior feeling of being correct quickly subsided as he pulled back the throttle and flew them out of the city.

CHAPTER 5

"Eden."

"What?"

"Get up."

"No."

Thiago grunted, shutting his eyes and reminding himself to tread lightly. He cracked his neck from side to side, still sore from spending a night in the pilot seat. After getting a wrapped package from his closet, he crossed over to where Eden was sleeping. Still dressed in her sweaty tank top and muddied jeans, she was lounging on his bed with her face buried in his pillows and her hands hanging off each side of the mattress. He placed the package next to her and awkwardly nudged her with his foot as if he were afraid of angering a wild beast.

"I didn't think you'd like the outfits TerraMates left you with, so I had something ordered before you arrived. You can wash off in the room next to you. Everything's labeled. If it's any consolation, I confirmed they sent the credits promised in your contract to your father's bank account. I can pull up the transaction for you later if you want. If you need anything else, I'll be in the cockpit."

Eden rose from the pillows. Her mouth stretched out in a wide yawn as Thiago headed down the steps and into the control room. Peeking over the railing, she saw Hercules by his scratching pole, his mouth smeared with blue juice as he slurped up a fruit. As she yanked over the package grumpily, she suddenly rubbed her stomach, blushing as it spewed inhuman noises announcing its neglect to anyone who would listen.

She grabbed a flask Thiago had thoughtfully put on the nightstand next to her. Drinking the contents to moisten her dry throat, she tore the package open, the tips of her toes curling in anticipation.

She pulled out three sets of clothes, noting with a sigh that there were a lot of jumpsuits on this planet. Chewing on her lip, she slipped on one of the coats. Her eyebrows shot up in surprise as the fabric became thinner than before. It was automatically adjusting to the temperature around her.

She felt happier as she vetted each article of clothing. Although it wasn't her usual style, it certainly wasn't anything close to the metal bikinis she had imagined. Still, it was too soon to tell Thiago's intentions. She wouldn't be letting her guard down.

Opting for one of the onyx-black jumpsuits, she headed into the bathroom.

"What's the name of this planet again?"

Thiago glanced over his shoulder. Eden was sliding into the cockpit. Fresh from the shower, her damp hair hung limply around her shoulders, still dripping lightly on the ends as she sat in the swiveling passenger's seat. Thiago reached for a peeled pomado fruit, tossing the neon-red, cube-shaped plant onto her lap.

"HT-007."

"That's a terribly ugly name." Eden crinkled her nose, sniffing the pomado. She bit into the fruit and nearly gagged at the unexpectedly bitter tang of the juices. Her face severely puckered, she exclaimed, "I'm pretty sure fruit's not supposed to taste like old diapers. What is it? Do people eat it?"

"Those are pomados. They're an acquired taste, but they'll fill you up nicely."

"Don't you have anything else around here that's edible? What I wouldn't give for some of my Dad's amazing mac-and-cheese right now."

"What's a mac-and-cheese?"

"It's one of the most significant culinary discoveries in America and on Earth. They're macaroni shells baked with thick, gooey cheese. Dad would cut up little hot dogs..."

"I have no idea what any of that is, but it all sounds revolting."

"Well, what would you know about it?"

"We're not scheduled to stop for another couple of hours," Thiago replied coolly, steering left on his controls. He popped open a compartment under the control panel and removed a large syringe with a thick needle. "I think I've got a few supplement packs somewhere around here. If you inject vitamins into your system, it should keep you going for at least a day."

"You've got to be kidding me. I'm not going to inject my food." Eden muttered under her breath and took another painful bite of the pomado. With Thiago's straight-faced, casual figure lingering in the corner of her eye, she couldn't keep the question that had been on her mind all night bottled in any longer.

"What are you, exactly?"

He grinned. "I'm half-Arkadian, half-human. Father and mother, respectively."

"Uh-huh," said Eden slowly. She tapped on her chin inquisitively. "Sorry, this is all a lot for me to process. I mean, on Earth we're still excited about finding liquid water on Mars. We're also in the grieving process for Pluto, which is no longer a planet."

"I'm impressed with your technological sophistication. Your Earthling governments must be doing a terrific job keeping you ignorant lot in the dark."

"Well, go ahead and enlighten me. What's going on here?"

Denying the pure enthusiasm coming from Eden was difficult. Thiago shifted in his seat and decided to start from the beginning.

"Over three hundred years ago, a group of Arkadian explorers stumbled onto this planet. Back then, the land was incredibly rich and fertile, and it contained massive mineral supplies of raw puranium. That's what we use in power plants and for fueling our shuttles and spaceships. A puranium rush took over the planet. Different alien colonies came in to get a piece of the puranium surplus. After a century, the minerals were bled dry, but more and more families remained to build communities. And here we are today."

"Fascinating," said Eden quietly, her brows knitted in thought. "Hang on a second. What did you mean when you said our governments were keeping us ignorant?"

"I cannot say with any certainty they have anything to do with TerraMates, but there's been intergalactic peace conferences with a few Earth representatives present."

"How many agencies are there, exactly?" asked Eden, her mouth going dry at the thought of all the helpless women smuggled to space over the years.

"Last I heard, TerraMates had over forty branches Earth-wide. I don't know how many of them work directly with the Noxx, but the branch that processed you certainly does."

"And who are the Noxx?"

Thiago motioned to the right, glancing out the windshield. He had suspended the craft about twenty feet above the docking station of a city. In broad daylight, the city was teeming with life. People moved around malls, office buildings, and various restaurants.

The lively atmosphere quickly changed as large spacecraft resembling army tanks hovered into view. Their ships, equipped with barbs, spikes, and rusted missile launchers, cast terrorizing shadows over the community before landing in front of the storefronts. Noxx officials climbed out of the ships, dressed in identical silver uniforms and armed with menacing weaponry strapped to their backs. Eden was appalled as she observed civilians fleeing away from the soldiers storming into the buildings. Hoping to prevent of a repeat of Eden's panic last night, Thiago flew away before the scene could get any uglier.

"They're the most notorious group of underground criminals on the planet. Their leader is Malatov, a demented dictator who controls most significant illegal operations on HT-007. Being born Noxx is a double-edged sword. You're practically untouchable by the law, but those that refuse to do Malatov's bidding and try to escape never make it far. They're very efficient."

"You sure know a lot about this stuff. Do you work for the police or something?"

"Hardly," Thiago laughed darkly. "I guess you could say I'm an independent contractor of sorts. There's a few of us out there. Some choose to work in groups, but I'm a solitary bounty hunter. Governments post notices about the large-scale criminals on the run they want to capture. I haul them in and collect the reward money."

"Well, that explains the aisle of weaponry you have going on back there. I'm slightly relieved. I mean, it sounds interesting," said Eden earnestly. She sighed, her shoulders sagging. "Listen, I'm still not sure what it is you want out of me. I don't know if you can tell, but I'm not exactly wealthy."

"No, you're poor. Judging by the state of your clothes, lack of jewelry, and your decision to step foot in TerraMates, I gathered as much."

"Wow, okay," said Eden, amused. "I guess you were born without a filter too, huh? Do you say everything that pops into your head?"

"I'm not sure what you mean," said Thiago, genuinely confused. "Why wouldn't I?"

"So you don't hurt other people, for one thing. Whoa. What's that?"

Eden gaped at the massive cemetery to their right. The land seemed to stretch on forever. It had many mounds of grass and simple gravestones. The majority were unmarked. Thiago didn't bat an eye and kept his eyes fixed straight out the window.

"It's the Land of the Fallen. It's an old graveyard. Most of the inhabitants are Noxx victims."

"It looks beautiful from up here," Eden whispered, without thinking through the connotations. Thiago wasn't the only one on the spaceship with filter issues. "Have you ever been there?"

"I visit the graves of my parents whenever possible."

"I'm sorry," said Eden in a hushed voice

"Why are you sorry? You didn't kill them. They were civilian casualties of a rogue bombing during a Noxx territory conflict war two decades ago."

Thiago could feel the marking on his forehead beginning to pound. It physically ached with the memories of his parents. He had intentionally pushed them aside to the corner of his mind for years. For the first time in ages, he could hear the throaty timbre of his father's laughter. He felt a fleeting sensation against a spot on his cheek his mother used to touch after he had played around in the dirt for hours.

"You loved your parents, didn't you?" asked Eden, realization gradually dawning on her. "I'm sorry, Thiago, I had no idea. You know, if you want to talk..."

The steering controls were suddenly slick with Thiago's sweat. Thiago's discomposure was growing increasingly evident as he yanked back on the levers. The pair was thrown back in their seats as the craft suddenly descended, making an unplanned landing. Thiago unstrapped himself from his seat and briskly headed out the cockpit.

"I don't want to talk. Sorry about this. I need to make a quick pit-stop. We're running low on supplies. I'll be right back."

CHAPTER 6

Eden bolted upright. Her eyelids were still heavy from her three-hour long nap. As she heard the droning hum of the spaceship, she realized they were already flying and on their way to the next destination. Her temples pulsed from the overabundance of sleep. "Great. Just great." Rubbing her temples, she swung her legs over Thiago's mattress and started down the steps, dragging her feet.

Hercules animatedly sprung out of his nest to greet her. He wouldn't let her go until she played with him. He wanted a few rounds of catch with a chew toy to start. Hercules only freed Eden after she had fussed over him sufficiently. Fondly giving the gentle giant a last rub on the noggin, Eden broke away from the lovable pet and entered the cockpit.

"Where are we going?" asked Eden innocently, sliding down into the passenger's seat.

"We're about to cross into the Blazian territory," Thiago answered her, giving her a small nod to acknowledge her presence.

"And what exactly are we doing there again?"

"I'm tracking down my next target. You're along for the ride," said Thiago, pulling up a profile on the dashboard screen. "This is Krypt. He's wanted for manufacturing and distribution of Xorxes, one of the most lethally addictive drugs on the planet. He's suspected of torturing

47

and killing family members and loved ones of addicts when they can't pay, but no one's come forward to testify against him."

"That's horrible. What a creep."

"He's scum all right, but scum with a big bounty. Low-lifes like him help put a roof over my head, so I can't complain."

"I'm glad it's all working out for you then," Eden snapped irritably. She reached inside her clothes. Her back itched, and she scratched it enthusiastically. Discovering a bumpy rash, she flared up, screeching, "What are these clothes made of?"

Thiago moved behind her and peered down her neck. His eyebrows raised as he noted, "It looks like your skin's sensitive to the new fabric."

"Oh, really? You think so?" Eden said sarcastically.

"Don't worry, it's a typical reaction on human skin, but it should go away in a day or two. You'll get used to it," said Thiago lightly. He was puzzled. "What's the matter with you now?"

"What do you think's the matter with me?" said Eden, throwing her hands up in frustration. "I feel like I've been abducted and taken hundreds of light-years away from home!"

"I understand that, but..."

"No, you don't," Eden sneered hatefully. Her eyes flashed. "In case you haven't noticed, I hate it here. The food's shitty, the clothes are itchy, and it always smells like feet. I can't be here forever. My dad's dying and Janine's by herself. I was the only one keeping our family together. What are they going to do without me?"

"Eden, I'm sorry."

"What will I do without them?" Eden whispered, lifting her legs onto the chair. Her glassy eyes drifted off to the side as she lost herself in thought and hugged her legs close to her body.

Thiago sighed, pulling a lever and starting the ship on a slow, fluid descent. He landed in a deserted area on the outskirts of Blazian territory. As Eden craned her neck to peek out the window, she wiped away her tears and frowned. Thiago's fingers breezed over a few switches on the control panel. Within seconds, the armor activated on the spaceship.

"I think we've gone far enough today. We can rest here tonight and get an early start tomorrow morning."

"Fine, whatever."

"Here," said Thiago, punching some buttons on his control board. A circular shutter on top of the screen split open, revealing a camera lens. "This will be pretty straightforward. Touch the red button once to record and again to stop. I'll find a way to get your message delivered to Earth."

"Really?" said Eden. Her heart swelled with hope.

"I'm going to head off to bed. Don't worry. I'll sleep on the ground floor, and you can take my bed again. Good night."

"Good night," said Eden. She watched as Thiago strode out of the cockpit.

"Janine?"

The distraught seventeen-year-old lifted her hands to push up the thick glasses slipping off the bridge of her nose. She looked similar to Eden, with a button nose and brilliant, long-lashed green eyes. The only thing that set them apart was Janine's silky, golden-blonde hair she usually had pulled up in a high ponytail. Now her hair was a disheveled mess as if she'd been running. Her chalk-white face was plagued with worry.

"Janine?" Eden gasped, reaching out to her, "What are you doing here?"

"Can you hurry? It's Dad. Things are bad. He needs you."

Eden's eyes darted around madly as she jumped to her feet and grabbed Janine's outstretched hand. Janine led her through a subway underpass. Eden yelped out in pain. Her fingers began to slip from her sister's as a faceless mass of aliens and enraged New Yorkers charged towards them. Since the flow of the mob elbowing past them was moving in the opposite direction, Eden felt herself being lifted off her feet. The crowd carried her backward against her will as Eden's mouth opened in a silent scream. Beads of sweat pooled at her temples from the strain.

"Eden! Come back! I need you too! Don't leave us!"

Eden pushed with all the force inside of her, but it wasn't enough. Her attempt to clamber over the shoulders of the moving crowd failed.

Eden twitched. The sheets under her were rustling. She turned over on her side, still half-asleep. As she found her face and hair once again matted with slime, she groaned. Her eyes snapped open, ready to fend off Thiago's over-affectionate pet.

"Not now Hercules!"

But it wasn't Hercules waking her up. When Eden opened her eyes, all she could see was a pair of blood-red eyes from a Blazian positioned inches from her face. He breathed down on her, the foul stench of death streaming out of his slitted nostrils.

CHAPTER 7

"Shit!"

As her breath froze in her throat, Eden desperately thrust her foot out from underneath her. She kicked the alien between his legs with all her might. As he fell back with a roaring groan, Eden rolled out from underneath him and flattened herself up against a corner. She groped for the pull chain to turn on the lights and yanked hard. Her eyes focused urgently as the overhead bulbs activated.

Eden's heart thudded against her chest like a rabid animal caged in a box. Thiago's ransacked room was in absolute disarray. The intruder had overturned chairs. Miscellaneous objects were escaping from open drawers.

Her darting eyes glanced back to the angry alien on the ground. He rocked back and forth as he cradled his crotch. Their eyes met across the room, and Eden felt her blood running cold. She watched as the alien reached out with his spindly arms and grabbed onto the side of a desk. He slowly pulled himself to his feet.

"I'm sorry?" Eden squeaked. Her throat scratched as she screamed at the dark floor below them. "Thiago! Hercules! Help!"

The Blazian lunged at her. His seemingly boneless limbs were stronger than she expected. Eden punched randomly as his fingers wrapped around her throat. His gray fingernails felt like brittle twigs as they pressed down on her neck. Barely flinching from Eden's assault, he smiled, revealing a gaping mouth with a smattering of jagged, blackened teeth. The pressure on Eden's windpipe made tears fall from the corners of her eyes. Her vision began to spin and blur.

A vicious thump sounded from the back of the intruder's head, and he instantly released his grip on Eden. The Blazian toppled backward and fell over the rail of the second floor, crashing onto the landing. Eden could hear a vicious snarl and the scurrying of multiple limbs from the pitch-black darkness of the first floor. The alien let out yelps of pain.

Thiago quickly glanced back at her over his shoulder before racing down the steps.

Massaging her throat, Eden wheezed as she swallowed gulps of refreshing air. She climbed down the steps cautiously, holding onto the wall for support. Her hands shook as she turned on the lights.

Even though the alien was taller than Thiago, he had lifted the assailant's feet inches off the floor, making him flail helplessly in the air. Eden gawked at the blood beginning to crust under the Blazian's noseless slits. His ill-fitting clothes clung to his frame in shreds, courtesy of Hercules. The exposed skin revealed blotches of discolored orange flesh. Thiago dragged the alien toward the door, grunting as he hurled the intruder out of the ship. The disoriented Blazian sprung to his feet, rocking from side to side as he bolted off, away from the madness.

Thiago massaged a kink in his neck. It gave off a satisfying crack as he flicked a switch on the door controls. A heavy metal door slid down from above to seal the gaping doorway. Leaning in to examine the switches, he made sure to key in a code twice, securing the lock. He turned around, shaking his head as he muttered.

"I don't believe I locked the door properly. I apologize."

Eden swung her arms around Thiago's neck and clung to him as she blubbered into his chest.

"Thank you," she sobbed, her eyes screwed shut. Inhaling the woodsy, soothing smell from his clothes, she cried into the fabric. "Thank you so, so much. I don't know what that thing would have done if you hadn't helped me."

"You're welcome," Thiago muttered hurriedly. Trying to avoid making a face at the snotty dampness on his shoulder, he attempted to wriggle away from her. "Wait, what's happening here?"

Hercules neighed in disapproval at Thiago, rolling all eight of its eyes. The animal clamped its opposable legs around itself to mime an embrace. Thiago stopped resisting and sighed. His free hand hung limply next to him as he stiffly patted down on her head with the other like he was burping a toddler.

"It will be okay," said Thiago. The feel of her thick hair was much softer than he'd imagined. "You'll live."

"That hurts," said Eden, ducking away from his mechanical patting. She blew away the strands of hair falling across her face. "Was that a Blazian? What's the use of having all these weapons if you're not going to use them?"

"To answer your first question, yes," Thiago replied, turning to scoop up the trash heaps Hercules was nudging toward him. "And there's no need for that. The weapons can cause extensive damage. I only use brute force to take down targets when it's necessary. He was just another junkie. They're typically harmless."

"Harmless, my ass," Eden grumbled, beginning to collecting fallen tin cups on the other side of the room. "I won't be inviting that snake-man to a party. Whoa. What's this?"

Eden picked up a tiny, clear vial wedged underneath the space of the kitchen countertop. She held it up to the light, mesmerized by a vibrant cobalt hue that appeared as she shook the grainy substance. As she started to open the vial, however, Thiago's hand appeared out of nowhere, slapping the bottle out of her palm.

"Hey!" said Eden indignantly. She scowled. "What in the world was that for?"

"Trust me. You don't want that stuff making contact with your skin, not even for a second," said Thiago. He checked the container. Eden trailed after him as he walked toward the bathroom.

"What is it?"

"Pure Xorxes crystals," said Thiago, dumping the vial into the toilet. He flushed it and raised his voice over the powerful vacuuming force of the bowl.

"You know what they say. Xorxes – not even once."

"I don't know what they say," said Eden, clapping a hand over her mouth to muffle her snorting. "Alien drugs?"

"Folks around here find it highly addictive. It's often used to fry mail-order bride brains into submission," said Thiago matter-of-factly as he closed the door behind him. "It must have fallen out of that junkie's pocket."

The amused grin vanished from Eden's face. She piped down immediately.

"That bastard was as high as the cosmos," Thiago explained. "We call them Fienders. They break into campsites and ships for drugs or any valuables they can pawn off. Unfortunately for this guy, I had neither of those things. The drug doesn't come cheap. A hit costs thousands of credits. It's ruined countless lives. My next target, Krypt, has a crew in charge of manufacturing most of the product around here."

"The gangster of your planet, I'm assuming," said Eden, clucking her tongue. "He sounds like a real asshole. I hope he gets what's coming to him."

"He will," Thiago promised, nodding his head. He glanced up at Eden, who was rinsing off cups and cutlery in the sink. She was yawning so much it looked like her mouth was stuck open. She whipped her stubbornly wild hair out of her face like she was evading a fly. The corners of his lips twitched. "You've had a rough night. You should go back to bed. I can get this cleaned up myself."

"Pleasesleepwithme," Eden suddenly blurted. An instant flush of red covered her cheeks.

Thiago couldn't believe what he thought he had heard. "What's that, now?"

Eden switched off the faucet. She took a deep breath as she nervously dried her hands on her pants.

"Sorry, that probably sounded different than what I intended. Would you mind if you slept up there with me tonight? It's your room, after all. I'm frightened of being in a new place, and I don't want to sleep alone this evening. You can say no if you don't want to, naturally."

"Slow down. You're getting all worked up over nothing," stated Thiago, raising an eyebrow. "I don't know how my presence will help you sleep, but sure, whatever. If that's what you require for a good night's rest, I'll sacrifice."

"Thanks," she whispered, flashing him a grateful smile. Her eyes landed on Hercules. His massive, fuzzy frame was curled up and fast asleep in a messy nest made from Thiago's scattered clothes. "We should get some rest. I think all of us are exhausted. I'll help you with this mess first thing in the morning."

Thiago followed Eden to his bedroom. He opened his closet doors, yanking out a pillow and a lumpy spare mattress. Swatting away the clouds of dusty neglect, he unrolled an old foam pad on the floor and started removing lumps with his fists.

"That old thing can't be good for your back," noted Eden from atop the bed, peering down at him. She untucked her crossed legs and stretched them out under her. "That's going to make your body ache, and that won't help you tomorrow. I've slept on my share of shitty mattresses. You can sleep up here if you'd like. I won't make it weird."

"I suppose so," said Thiago, tossing the mattress back in the closet and joining her. The bed shifted under his weight as he reached over to turn off the glaring light above them. "I'll see you in the morning."

"Thanks again, Thiago," said Eden. The bed creaked as she turned from him and snuggled into her pillow.

"Good night."

"Good night."

Thiago turned to his side and away from her. The buzzed side of his hair sank into the coolness of his pillow. He closed his eyes. Just as he was beginning to lose himself in the darkness of slumber, he felt the smooth, cold touch of Eden's foot graze against his calf. Stirring, he lifted his head off his pillow and stared at the rhythmic snoring body behind him. The bundle of Eden lay perfectly still. One leg jutted out behind her like a snoozing flamingo.

He fell back on his pillow. When he hooked his toe between the spaces of her foot, his warmth absorbed her coldness. With the faintest hint of a smile playing on his lips, Thiago's eyelids closed again. The mark on his forehead briefly glowed before he drifted off into a deep, dreamless sleep.

CHAPTER 8

A few hours after Thiago woke up, Eden opened her eyes to the familiar sound of the spacecraft taking flight. She took a quick shower and slipped into her jumpsuit. The glittery red fabric automatically adjusted itself to the contours of her body. After she had dressed, she descended the stairs to the first floor of the ship. There was no evidence of the break-in last night. In fact, the craft never looked better. It appeared the Blazian's late-night intrusion had prompted a round of overdue spring cleaning.

"Good morning," Eden greeted Thiago as she entered the cockpit. She threw her hair forward and wrapped a towel around her loose hair, tucking the knot inside the towel turban.

"It's hardly morning. The sun's almost down already," Thiago informed her. He wrinkled his nose, wiping off his neck. Her hair had splashed him with a drizzle of water. "I was just about to wake you. I'm stopping by the Jova Tavern to pick up some dinner and a pint of Pasquin ale. Would you like me to get you anything?"

"Why don't I come with you?"

Thiago threw his head back in hearty laughter. The marking on his forehead glowed briefly, and he turned toward Eden. His smile disappeared when he saw the stone cold look on her face.

"You're serious. I'm sorry to say that is a bad idea."

"And why not?" Eden demanded, narrowing her eyes in a challenge. "Are you telling me I'm going to be trapped here for the rest of my life? Do you plan to treat me as if I'm a monster chained up in the attic?"

"I think you're a bit dramatic," Thiago said calmly, his thick, flaxen brows raised.

"I don't know about that." Eden tapped her chin for emphasis. "One, I'm one of countless intergalactic human trafficking victims, which has been going on for God knows how long. Two, I was beamed hundreds of lightyears away from Earth and my family to an unknown planet. Three, my husband's an alien!"

Thiago coughed.

"I'm sorry, half-alien. I'm not dramatic at all. I think I'm rather calm."

"Half-Arkadian. The aliens here don't like it when people treat them as a single group. We consider it racist."

"Forgive me for being politically incorrect," Eden shot back sarcastically. Breathing heavily from the conclusion of her outburst, she realized she felt better after releasing her burdens. "You know what? I'm sorry. I keep biting your head off. You can't imagine the stress I'm under right now."

Eden jolted slightly in her seat as Thiago guided the ship to a bumpy landing. She squinted through the storm of dust settling beneath the windshield. Her heart sank as

Thiago disappeared from the cockpit without saying a word.

"Hang on a second. Where are you going?" She must have really made him upset this time. It wasn't as if she was crabby for fun. But even if she was, who could blame her?

"Here – put these on."

She glanced up in surprise as Thiago reappeared in the doorway of the cockpit. He handed her a padded, floor-length cloak made from scales. It had a strong, distinctive smell. Motioning for her to remove her slippers, he gave her a cute pair of boots with platform soles. He clicked a minuscule button on the side, adding an extra three feet to their height. Eden's eyes bulged in disbelieving wonder as she stared at the shoes.

"Don't worry. They're self-balancing," said Thiago, as if reading Eden's mind. He quickly unbuckled the boots. "Hurry up, then. You wanted to come along, didn't you?"

"Yes!" exclaimed Eden. She unwrapped a white, featureless mask from the cloak and pulled it over her face as her slender figure vanished in the dark cape. "Thank you."

"Keep your hood on at all times and don't remove the mask for any reason. Not even once. It might get hot in there, but you need to cover yourself if you want to go out. These folks here don't take kindly to humans running around on the loose. Do we understand each other?"

"Of course. I'll remember."

"Good. Let's go."

"I never imagined a place like this existed in the universe."

Eden deeply exhaled as she stood in the entryway of the tavern, her round eyes shining. The massive front door slammed into her butt as it swung shut, knocking her forward and nearly off-balance. The interior of the building was much larger than it appeared from the outside. Foggy, bluish-green lighting illuminated various bustling food stalls on the sides. In between were clusters of bar tables and private booths throbbing with lively chatter and inebriated merriment.

Thiago was leading them toward an oval-shaped bar. As she tagged along behind him, she surveyed the patrons with curiosity. They were mainly drunken Blazians, with a sprinkling of other alien races she couldn't identify yet.

"Thirsty?" asked Thiago, handing her a fizzy purple drink in a glass shaped like a double-stranded DNA molecule. "It's pomado-honeyberry pop. There's not a big selection. It's the only non-alcoholic drink they have."

Eden took a hesitant sip. She grinned as she chugged back half the syrupy-sweet, tangy contents of the glass. "That was delicious."

"You like that garbage?" said Thiago incredulously, shaking his head. "Why am I surprised? Do you want to take a look at the menu? I can show you some more mainstream choices."

Eden wasn't listening to him. She focused on something directly over his shoulder. Thiago looked behind him at a group of elderly Blazians slowly trudging up the steps of the stage and taking positions familiar to them. The silver-haired aliens smiled toothless grins, waving at the whistling crowds. The snazzily dressed quintet unpacked oddly-shaped equipment, including sharp string instruments, rounded harmonicas, and an accordion with glowing keys.

The frontman tapped a cymbal on his hat to start them off while the rest of the band nodded along. On cue, a powerful wave of electric bluegrass swept the tavern, bringing the entire room to their feet. A group of voluptuous Blazians and alien women with sparkling piercings all over their bodies sauntered toward the dance floor with their partners. Eden lifted an eyebrow. Trashy dancing was recognizable everywhere in the universe. She watched curiously as curvy aliens ground their privates against each other.

"They're unbelievable!" Eden shouted over the music, cupping her hands over her mouth.

"The Khula Brothers have been around for over a century. They're something of an underground legend around here. Forget them. We don't have a lot of time."

Seeing the look of joy in her eyes, Thiago groaned under his breath.

"Stay here and finish the rest of the song. I'm going to pick out some food for us. I'll be right back. Don't move a muscle and don't do anything that comes naturally to you. Don't attract any attention whatsoever."

"Got it. I'm invisible," Eden muttered, pushing him away. "I'll have whatever you're having, thanks."

Thiago cut through the crowd and into an eatery on the opposite side of the tavern. Eden leaned back against the bar, lifting her mask to drain the rest of her drink. The rumbling burp from the shadows of her hood was thankfully drowned out by the energetic music. She raised her empty glass and swayed along to the beat. A group of drunken Blazian women elbowed their way to the front of the crowd and ripped open their tops to flash the band, earning a roar of raucous approval from the rest of the patrons.

Though Eden found herself wholeheartedly relishing the fun songs, she couldn't help but feel a faint tug on her heartstrings. She began to recall all the times her father would play his Ricky Skaggs bluegrass collection in their beat-up station wagon before the creditors repossessed it. Eden sat in the front and her younger sister Janine claimed the entire backseat. The Castle trio had memorized the words to every song and sang on the drive home from school. They weren't always in the correct key, but they made up for it with enthusiasm. That was, of course, before cancer rendered their father bedridden and helpless.

The bittersweet memory faded into another. Eden pictured the pale face of her younger sister. Janine had just acquired her driver's license. The second-hand Nissan she'd worked so hard to save for was now used to drive their father to and from his chemo appointments instead of the usual carefree activities of a 17-year-old.

Eden hoped the money from TerraMates would benefit her family during her unexplained absence.

Eden swallowed, blinking furiously in an attempt to snap herself out of her daze. As the song came to an end, the crowd exploded in wild applause, hoping for an encore. She had a big smile on her face and raised her glass again to whoop along with the audience. In her enthusiasm, she started pumping her fist in the air, accidentally colliding with the massive patron behind her.

She whirled around to apologize, only to have the blood drain from her face, making her natural pallor match the shade of her blank mask. A muscular Noxx official in army fatigues glowered at her, the slimy scales on his ghost-white face dripping with the colored liquor from his empty glass. Eden had made the alien spill his drink on himself.

The Noxx sized her up, breathing heavily through his flared nostrils like an angry bull seeing the movements of the matador's cape. The milky, bright feathers on his head open simultaneously with the webbed wings on his back. He was preparing for combat. The patrons around them dispersed with startling speed.

Eden set her glass down on the bar and raised her palms defensively, retreating slowly. Before the alien could move any closer to Eden, Thiago appeared by her side, wielding a bar stool. He broke it over the official's head. Taken by surprise, the Noxx reeled backward and fell onto the floor, surrounded by fragmented stool splinters. The tavern flared up in blind-punching, table-flipping chaos. The band played on, providing a suitable soundtrack to the hysteria. Thiago and Eden crept out of the establishment in the frenzy.

"I thought I said don't draw attention. I left her for five minutes. That was a Noxx official. She must be out of her damn mind." Thiago polished off his grilled kobaru and grains bowl, muttering to himself grumpily under his breath between mouthfuls.

"I'm right here, you know," Eden reminded him from the passenger's seat. She lowered her eyes, trying to apologize again. "It was an accident. I'm sorry. I understand if you don't want me to leave the ship ever again."

"I never said that," said Thiago with a sigh. "We'll just have to stay with each other from now on. And I strongly recommend you never venture out of here unsupervised."

"Thanks, Thiago," said Eden, smiling weakly. "I won't."

"Good. We'll test your understanding right away."

Eden gripped the edge of the dashboard for support as the ship landed in a clearing several feet from an abandoned warehouse. Thiago emptied his goblet and rose from his seat, striding out of the cockpit. Eden followed him, her mouth slightly open. She watched as Thiago strapped a thick belt over his shoulder and filled the slots with sharp daggers, glinting restraints, and other weaponry she didn't recognize.

"Are you leaving right now?"

"We're close to Krypt's warehouse. Hercules is coming with me to take down the target. I've programmed the shields to activate as soon as we leave. You should be safe here."

"That doesn't sound reassuring. How long should I wait for you before I start to worry?"

"It depends," said Thiago vaguely, shrugging. "I shouldn't be long. Do you know what to do?"

"I know, I know. Stay right here."

"Good. We'll see you soon."

Thiago gave her a final nod before hopping off the ship with Hercules tailing closely behind him. As soon as the front door sealed shut, Eden heard the metallic cranking of several locking mechanisms turning on. The shielded craft was now impenetrable.

CHAPTER 9

Eden chewed on the last of her pulled kobaru meat. It tasted like grilled chicken in a savory sauce. As she dabbed at her lips with a leaf-textured napkin, she touched a screen on the dashboard. It was the only instrument on the ship she felt comfortable using. She wasn't sure when Thiago and Hercules would return. For entertainment, she had begun reading about Thiago's former and future targets.

There was a profile of a sadistic rapist and murderer with a male call-boy fetish. A Leudanese named Kronka had evaded authorities with a decade-long killing spree before Thiago captured him. She shuddered at the moving mugshot of a two-headed creature with gouged-out eye sockets, clawing menacingly at the camera.

The scorned Dartian princess Briaisha went on a vigilante crusade against unfaithful husbands. She disemboweled her victims and left their entrails packaged in a gift-wrapped basket on their wives' doorsteps. Over 30 wives were graced with Briaisha's gifts before Thiago stopped her.

Galvantor, brother of the Noxx leader, Malatov, was a 'free-spirit' who started a personal doomsday cult. The Paradise Achievers saw twenty thousand misguided families perish in synchronized suicide after consuming drinks laced with lethal doses of poison. Somehow Galvantor did not imbibe his deadly concoction and remained on the run for over twenty-five years before Thiago hauled the emaciated and disgraced leader to the authorities.

She couldn't believe Thiago had singlehandedly taken these horrifying criminals out of space. It was no wonder he was cranky. He must have seen horrors that could not be imagined by the sickest minds.

She found herself filled with a sense of revulsion at the criminals and admiration for Thiago. His bounties weren't petty-thieving, substance-possessing jokes. They were a danger to the universe.

Eden glanced down at her watch. They had been gone for almost an hour now. Could this be normal? Her brows furrowed as she anxiously gnawed on her lip. What if this was the first mission he failed? Were they were hurt? Or worse? A hundred questions raced through her mind, each more erratic than the next.

She jumped up from her seat and ran to the windows, hoping to catch a glimpse of Thiago. She found every opening sealed with the shield's protective, steel-gray shell.

Eden turned back to the cockpit, seating herself on the pilot's seat. She began to play around with the controls, hoping to lower the shield. Every time Eden made a mistake, a noise sounded, signaling an access error and increasing her frustration. With an exasperated sigh, she pounded down with her fists, striking the screen and knocking over a striped yellow lever to her right.

There was a sharp sound of alert as all the shields on the craft retracted. Eden bounced off her seat immediately. She gazed out of the windshield, squinting out at her surroundings. Night had fallen, and darkness covered the land. They were in a clearing bordered by stretches of land covered with tall trees. The gnarled branches were abundant with fern-like leaves in earthy, purplish tones. They rustled in the breeze like a puppeteer controlled them.

Wiping away the sweat snaking down her cheeks, she strode out of the cockpit toward the armory. She chose something that looked dangerous – a small, bazooka-shaped weapon that was heavier than it appeared. Grabbing a club for good measure, she moved toward the exit and stepped onto the pedal under the wall, revealing an opening in the spaceship. She moved through the egress before the doors of the craft clamped shut behind her.

Traces of her breath slipped past her lips and left clouds in the cold of the night. Gravel and dried leaves crunched under her boots as she walked along a path in the quiet glade. Eden spied muted light beyond a thicket of lopsided trees. She headed west from the craft toward the only illumination she could see.

Eden hid behind an unusually thick trunk, her hammering heart making it difficult to hear anything. The enormous double-story warehouse was hard to miss sitting in the middle of the woods. She narrowed her eyes to get a better look, counting four immobile figures sprawled out across the entryway. Her legs were the consistency of wobbly gelatin. Eden approached the bodies with the caution of a delinquent teenager sneaking past their snoozing parents in the living room. She lifted her legs cautiously, stepping over the unconscious figures of three Blazian guards and a Noxx official.

The warehouse lights were smashed and dangled from their fixtures. Twinkling pools of Xorxes crystals spilled out from large vats tipped onto their sides. Clouds of creamy smoke sputtered over the tables, emerging from cracks in complicated sets of glass tubes and beakers.

Eden's ears perked up at the sound of Hercules' distinctive distress squeals. They were coming from the second floor. Incapacitated bodies obstructed her path, but she leaped over them like an Olympian jumping over hurdles. She clambered up the steps clumsily, clutching her weapons tightly against her chest. She froze when she reached the landing.

Hercules was staving off a horde of five Blazian cronies. He had seized one by the neck with his pincers. The creature swung the flailing Blazian toward his companions, sweeping them off their feet like a row of dominoes.

Krypt paced around the room as if he was hunting for something. He was instantly recognizable. He wore a velvet, maroon suit that made him look superior to his men. Eden spotted Thiago crouched under a table. His kept his head down as he reloaded one of his weapons. Her palms became slick with sweat. She watched in terror as Krypt closed in on Thiago. The creature's fingers curled around the edge of Thiago's table. He was about to flip it over.

"Oh no – Thiago!"

Eden shuffled forward, the club dropping onto the ground next to her. She raised her weapon and aimed at Krypt. One trembling hand closed around the grip while her finger curled around the trigger. Her heart fluttered when she fired.

A deafening boom erupted from the mouth of her weapon. A bolt of blue lightning narrowly missed Krypt's ear, striking and utterly shattering all the glass in the windowpanes behind him. The delayed kickback of Eden's weapon sent her hurtling backward and crashing onto the pillars behind her.

Her body was flat against the ground. Eden lifted her head sluggishly. She saw two copies of Krypt's blurry silhouette weave toward the stairs and exit the room.

"Thiago," she croaked, attempting to signal him with a limp wrist. "He's getting away."

A cloud of red filled Eden's vision. A warm trickle of blood started to flow out her ears, and she fell back to the ground.

CHAPTER 10

"My head hurts."

Eden peeled back her eyelids slowly. Her head throbbed like angry woodpeckers were drilling at her temples. Rubbing her face above the nose, she hefted herself off the ground. She had been lying on a mattress on the cold cockpit floor of Thiago's ship. She looked down at herself and gasped at a sharp jab that shot through her ribs.

She wore a black robe with a warm, woolen lining. Someone had bandaged her waist and left arm with a breathable brown cloth. The bandages didn't cover all her wounds. She had other scratches around her body. A bright pink salve coated her scratches; it felt cool when she touched it.

Most of the scratches looked superficial. Even the deepest wound running across her stomach was nearly healed already.

She glanced over to her right at the cockpit. The spaceship was on auto-pilot, steering itself through the surreal imagery of rolling clouds tinted with the rising sun's rusty amber hues. Thiago sat in the driver's seat, hunched over the screen and looking at his dashboard.

"Hi," said Eden, shrugging the robe off her shoulders to look at the cuts on her back. "How long was I out?"

Fully absorbed with the profile of his next target, Thiago didn't answer her.

"Hello? Thiago?" said Eden, her forehead wrinkling in annoyance. She twisted her lips thoughtfully. "Holograms aren't a thing here, are they?" "

The sound of a heavy object hitting something repeatedly rang against the steel floors beneath them. Stools and tables around the ship rattled from the hits. A cupboard door swung open from a particularly hard blow. Eden shrank up against the wall of the vessel instinctively. She slid up to the side, peeking out the window of the cockpit door. She didn't see anything unusual. Hercules, however, circled an old rug centered on the floor, snapping his pincers and growling.

"What was that?"

"Your mouth seems to be working fine. Relax," said Thiago stonily, without lifting his eyes from the screen. "He's properly restrained and encased in a 2-meter thick slab of concrete. He can try to escape, but no one's ever managed to break out of our cell."

Eden's eyes widened in sudden realization. "Are you out of your mind? Is Krypt under us? How did you do that? Never mind. I thought we might have giant space termites."

"These low-lifes have to be transported to the authorities one way or another. They won't come aboard my ship willingly."

"I guess you're right. I never thought about it," Eden muttered, grumpily tying her robe around her waist. "I feel like things are getting a little tense here, so I'm just

75

going to go upstairs and cool off. I'm glad you and Hercules are okay."

"We are. No thanks to you."

"What was that?" said Eden, stopping midway to the cockpit doors. "I don't think I caught your meaning."

Thiago glanced over his shoulder at her. He was puzzled, but he could follow directions. "I wasn't whispering, and I think my intentions were clear. Did you not hear me? I said, no thanks to you."

"I know what you said!" Eden snapped. "I wasn't looking for a thank you or anything for having your back out there in that gross, old warehouse, but at the very least, you could not blame me."

"Why would I thank you? You broke your word and came running after me when I explicitly told you not to. You had no training and no plan. I'm beginning to doubt if you people on Earth were born with common sense. That was wildly irresponsible. Krypt might have killed you."

"Not only was I in the martial arts club in high school, but I've also completed a total of three hour-long self-defense classes as an adult. It's not like you aliens are any better," Eden shot back, one hand firmly planted on her hips. She raised her voice over Krypt's floor-shaking antics in the other room. "You're all surly and ungrateful, and I was born and bred in New York City! I don't know how Hercules stays sweet and cuddly after hanging around you all day. I didn't see you for over an hour. What was I supposed to do? I was worried sick."

"I had everything under control until you showed up."

"From where I was standing, it sure looked like Krypt was about to maul your head."

"Shut up!" roared Eden and Thiago in unison, glaring heatedly at each other.

Beep. Beep. Beep.

They turned their attention to the windshield, currently overlaid with a grid map and blinking red coordinates. The craft began a smooth, slow descent. The floor rumbled as the spaceship released its wheels and hovered over the landing strip of a pod suspended above the ground. Behind the landing strip was a prestigious government building. It was grandly regal in contrast to the heavily-manned prison guard towers and drab walls surrounding it, garnished with spikes that expelled threatening sparks.

Eden muttered to herself as she followed Thiago out of the cockpit. "Stay back," Thiago warned.

He grabbed onto the edge of his wall of weapons and lifted it over his head, revealing an extra storage space stuffed with broken junk. Casually throwing a few objects over his shoulder, he reached in and pulled out a rectangular wooden box with an antenna loop protruding from the side. He swung the pivoting wall down and set the box onto a podium. He lifted the cover of the yellow switch next to his weapons, retreating as the floorboards pulled back.

Eden gawked as a horizontal cell raised from the ground. Krypt lay flat on his back, his wrists restrained with a unique set of strong black handcuffs. There was a metal contraption fitted over his head like a middle schooler's over-engineered headgear. His flashing eyes balefully monitored every one of Thiago's movements, bits of frothing drool collecting on the sides of his mouth.

Thiago remained composed even as Krypt began hurling obscenities in his direction. He proceeded to fiddle with some knobs and twisted out the other antenna of the rectangular device to its fullest.

Raising his hand like a conductor, he waved a hand in front of the antenna. A haunting, high-pitched note emitted from the instrument. The beautifully serene chord was received with equally intense animosity as Krypt cried out in his cage, writhing in his headgear.

"That was on the lowest setting. We can do this all day. Or you can choose to cooperate and make this easy for both of us. We'll walk into headquarters together, and you can keep the dignity you have remaining. I'll drop you off at the office, collect my credits and be on my merry way. Which will it be?"

Krypt turned away from Thiago. A hateful look in his eyes was still present, but subdued. The criminal focused on a stain on the floor next to him. Thiago flashed a triumphant smile, nodding.

"Wise choice," said Thiago, keying in a security code to unlock the cage. He stepped aside just in time to avoid a collision as Krypt pitched forward. Shaking his head, he helped the criminal to his feet as Hercules bared his pincers from the sidelines. "Hurry up now, off you go."

As Eden opened the front door, Krypt lumbered past her, leering one last time before ducking his head under the doorway and exiting the craft. Thiago slung a navy-blue satchel over his shoulder, turning back to Eden before slipping out the door.

"I'll be back in half an hour. 45 minutes at most. If I'm not back in 46, don't worry. Stay put!"

"Could you be more annoying? Get out of here!" Eden rolled her eyes as the door sealed shut in Thiago's grinning face.

She winced as she felt a hot, stabbing sensation on her back. Her wounds had not healed as much as she thought. Holding onto her back with one hand, she wandered into the kitchen for something to cure her hunger and take her mind off her pain. Hercules trotted along behind her, happily wagging its broad, forked tongue.

"Are you hungry?" Eden cooed. She ruffled the top of Hercules' head, the creature purring agreeably under her touch. "I'm hungry too. Let's raid your master's cupboards and see if he's got anything edible around here."

She retrieved a dusty, half-open box of what appeared to be alien cereal. The box had a picture of colorful marshmallows shaped like tiny, sweet humans. When she opened the box, a whiff of mold and neglect waved into her face. She swiftly dumped the box in the trash, fanning out the air in front of her.

"Bachelors," gagged Eden, rolling her eyes. Hercules nudged her from the back, guiding her forward. "What's up, Herc?"

The creature led her in front of a small oven, blinking back at her expectantly. She unhooked the latch of the oven door, pulling out a tray. She felt her chest warming at the baked dish waiting for her. It looked suspiciously like macaroni and cheese, only the homemade macaroni shells were as purple as yams, marinating in a green sauce. An extra coating of crispy, edge-burnt cheese lay on top of it.

"Did he make this for me?"

Hercules nodded in reply, beckoning her toward the refrigerator with its hairy legs. Eden opened the fridge, a gasp of astonishment lodging in her throat. The top two shelves of the fridge contained cans of pomado-honeyberry pop. Unable to suppress a smile any longer, she beamed to herself, grabbing a soda can and cracking open the tab.

"Are you saying I'm a little too harsh on him? Or is he making it difficult for me to leave?"

Hercules made a small noise, raising four of its legs as if to shrug at her. Eden grabbed the dish and reached for the cleanest utensil she could find before joining the creature in its nest. She tucked her legs underneath her and rested her head against the warmth of Hercules' torso. Unleashing a long, drawn-out sigh, she began to dig into the dish.

CHAPTER 11

Thiago listened thoughtfully to the poignantly melodious tune wafting out of his spaceship. He tiptoed through the front door, treading lightly toward Eden as he watched her. Seemingly oblivious to his arrival, she had her back turned to him. She sat on a stool in front of a rectangular device. Her fingers wiggled gracefully in mid-air, plucking invisible strings from a vertical antenna. Thiago folded his arms over his chest and leaned back against the wall, a floorboard creaking under the weight of his boots.

"Oh," said Eden, jumping back in her seat. The look of alarm on her face quickly changed to one of relief. "I didn't hear you come in."

"You don't have to stop," said Thiago softly, clearing his throat. "That is, if you don't want to."

"Sorry, I didn't mean to touch your stuff," Eden mumbled, an embarrassed flush of pink creeping into her cheeks. "I got bored. There's not much to do around here."

"It's fine," said Thiago earnestly, stroking his chin. "You're excellent. Did you compose that piece yourself?"

"I wish," snorted Eden.

Thiago found himself staring as she gathered her unruly mass of copper hair over one side of her neck, exposing a thin sliver of her porcelain flesh. She started up the song once more. This time, she kept her eyes closed, allowing her head to rock back and forth to the music.

"This is a Louis Armstrong classic called 'West End Blues.' It's one of only two songs I know how to play on a guitar," Eden explained. She stopped playing abruptly, smiling as she turned back to face him. "And that's all I know. What do you call this instrument?"

"It's a theremin. Ironically, it's a device from Earth. I believe a Russian physicist created it. I'm not sure how it made its way from Earth to space, but I retrieved it from an old junkyard and tinkered with it until I got it to work."

"Interesting," said Eden slowly, rising to help Thiago dismantle the device. She ran a tongue over her lips thoughtfully, clearing her throat as she handed him the pieces to stow away behind the arsenal. "Thanks for the food, by the way. It was tasty despite the appearance. I'm not sure if the burnt edges were intentional, but it was just like Dad used to make it."

"No problem. I followed a recipe I found from your home planet. It wasn't yellow, but I did what I could."

"It tasted fantastic," said Eden gently, playing with the wrinkled creases on her elbows. "It was sweet."

"I'm pretty sure it was meant to be a savory dish."

"I meant, what you did was sweet. You know, like all the 'garbage' sodas you bought for me in the fridge."

"I ordered everything in one sitting and had it delivered," Thiago said hastily. He had hardly ever received praise from those around him and he was growing increasingly uncomfortable. "Besides, you're too stubborn to drink anything other than that toxic swill. I didn't want to come home to find you starved to death and staining my floors."

"Oh, right. Sure," laughed Eden, punching him playfully on the arm. She fell back on a large cushioned armchair. Thousands of microscopic alien creatures in individual bean casings shifted under her weight. They swarmed together, massaging the tension out of her back through the fabric of the chair. "I think I'm growing on you."

"You're welcome to think whatever you'd like," said Thiago tonelessly. He grabbed a jug of Pasquin ale from the cabinet above him and poured a shot into a clean goblet.

As he guzzled down the bitter liquor, Eden stood up. She crossed the kitchen and moved to the kitchen countertop next to Thiago. He was facing away from her. Wordlessly, she inspected the aged scars on the side of his neck. One ragged scar appeared to stretch down his back, disappearing from the neckline of Thiago's hooded jumpsuit. Biting down on her tongue, she traced the mark with her fingertip.

Thiago shivered at the unexpected contact, turning back questioningly. "Hey!"

"Did you get this from the warehouse, or is it an old battle scar?"

"I guess you could say it was my first. It turns twenty-four this year," said Thiago glumly.

"Can I see it?" said Eden, her mossy-green eyes widening.

"What? What for?" Thiago asked. Noting the adamant expression on Eden's face, he grudgingly agreed. He unzipped his jumpsuit from the waist, shedding off the top half of his outfit and casting it aside. Eden was taken aback by the ripples of muscle in his naked upper body, sculpted naturally by years of strenuous bounty hunting. Her diverted eyes roamed back to his scar. The flesh-toned wound stopped halfway down his spine.

"Hang on a minute. Twenty-four years ago? You were just a kid."

"I was nine."

"The bombing from the Noxx territory wars was twenty years ago," Eden whispered. Her chest tightened. "What happened?"

"Like you said, it happened over twenty years ago. There's no sense in bringing it up now."

"I'm not going anywhere."

"Fine, if you insist. We used to live out in the countryside, in an area called Myron Plains. There were a few hundred or so families, mostly similar to mine — husbands who'd fallen for their human mail-order brides and decided to start families of their own. Our unique family dynamic wasn't accepted or tolerated by society, which was why we were living in the country outskirts."

Eden listened intently. She watched as she saw a fleeting look of vulnerability cross Thiago's steely composure.

"My mother was making sweet bread in the kitchen. My father was out in the yard sharpening handmade tools he traded with other villagers in Myron. I'd just completed one of the passages my mother assigned to me, so I ran outside to play. I went to a creek I visited every day. I remember leaning over the bank of the river, playing with a couple of baby anuras. Out of nowhere, a blaring sound filled the air. All the anuras swam away from me for cover faster than I'd ever seen them move before."

"Oh no," Eden breathed, her stomach twisting as she braced herself.

"There was an explosion of course, but I barely remember it. The next thing I knew, I was washed up on the bank of a creek about thirty miles south from where I'd started. I still don't know how I managed to survive the blast. I wandered for days but eventually hiked back to my town. Everyone I knew was dead. They completely obliterated Myron. We made it into a graveyard shortly after."

"The Land of the Fallen," said Eden morosely, tugging at the sleeve of her robe.

"Right," said Thiago, averting his eyes. He cleared his throat, downing the rest of the ale and chucking his goblet into the sink.

Thiago hadn't thought about the incident for over two decades, but it was always lurking at the corner of his mind, waiting to take over his thoughts. The memory started a wave of dormant emotions flowing through his body. Like everything that discomforted him that wasn't a physical problem, he tried to flush it out of his system. Thiago took a deep, revitalizing breath, swallowing a tickle building up in his throat.

"I'm sorry," Eden murmured, her voice thick with emotion.

Her fingers gingerly scraped down the length of his scar, feeling his shoulders tensing up under her wandering touch. There were no more words to say, but her chest swelled with the burning desire to ravage his deliciously firm body and take away his pain. She resisted her urge. Instead, she closed in on his rigid back, planting a line of softly sensual kisses along the length of his scar.

Thiago spun around without warning, his hands smoothly circling her waist and pulling her close to him. Eden's surprised giggles trailed off timidly as the distance between his strikingly handsome face and hers dwindled. He cupped his hands around her chin and kissed her, delicately dragging down her bottom lip against his.

Eden moaned, sinking into the kiss. As their lips collided, her hands traveled up and over the back of his head. The patterns on his shaved head felt bristly against her palms. His groping hands slid down her back and found their way to her butt. He smirked, awarding himself a hearty grab as he hoisted Eden off the floor and wrapped her legs around his waist.

The pair continued to kiss as he carried her past a napping Hercules asleep in its nest. They teetered up the flight of steps, knocking sideways into the wall and railing before making it up the landing. Thiago gently placed her slender frame onto his bed. Eden's robe came undone as she toppled backward, the globes of her milky, bare breasts jiggling into view. She made a face, rubbing on her bandaged waist.

"Be gentle. I'm injured, remember?"

"Sorry." The impish grin on Thiago's face weakened Eden's legs. He climbed into bed and crawled on top of her. The back of his hands graced the supple bottom curves of her pear-shaped breasts. With his intense gaze steadily fixed on hers, his lips latched onto her nipple. She moaned, feeling herself hardening in his mouth as his tongue swirled around her.

"When I was bandaging you today, it took all the restraint I had to refrain from looking at your body."

Her appreciative whimpering was stifled while she chewed her lip. Squirming against the wrinkled sheets, she snatched his taunting hands and slapped them roughly onto her breasts. With her fingers interlaced through the gaps of his fervently kneading hands, she positioned her legs around him. The sole of her foot moved against his cock bulging through his jumpsuit. Her toes wriggled as she pressed down and began to move her foot in circular motions.

"You better do something about that before I do."

Eden flashed him a quick wink, deliberately licking the ruby red of her lips. Thiago stripped off the rest of his jumpsuit and flung it behind him, sending the pair of pants flying over the second-floor railing. As he stood at the foot of the bed, Eden crept toward him, her breasts swaying slightly from side to side. She wrapped her fingers around the thick girth of his cock and steered it into her mouth. As his tip touched the back of her throat, she gagged slightly, titillated tears springing to the corners of her eyes.

Eden pulled away from him, discarding her bathrobe and panties onto the floor. She climbed back into bed on all fours, turning away from him. With her fleshy, bubble-shaped ass ready and poised in midair, she shifted her legs further apart. As Thiago eyed the moist gleam of pink blinking at him from her shifting legs, his cock pulsed in his hands. Slathering a palmful of spit over his erection, he mounted her from behind, teasing the tip of his pole with the slickness of her invitingly warm crevice.

Slowly, Thiago eased himself through the tightness of her folds. Eden whipped back her head, her fiery hair cascading over her shoulders. Her pussy nursed him as he pumped in and out of her. She tightly gripped the sheets to keep herself standing upright and her knees from buckling underneath her. Thiago had his hand fastened to her waist, the other caressing the jumping spheres of her soft breasts.

Beads of sweat poured down the canvas of Thiago's back like raindrops racing to the bottom of a windowsill. Eden's moans increased as he reached around to tweak the delicate pearl above her folds. Her back arched on the rocking bed, a look of turbulent delight unfolding across her face. She felt her toes curling as her juices gushed over Thiago, who was still drilling in and out of her.

Sensing the closeness of his release, Thiago dismounted. Eden's lanky, feminine physique crumbled across the bed, a sensation of numbness crawling up her legs. She watched as Thiago guided his creamy emissions onto a pile of his clothes on the floor. A golden glow flickered across the arrows intersecting the U-marking on his forehead. As quick as the light came, it vanished, disappearing at the end of his release.

Thiago rolled his head around his neck as he picked up his clothes and stuffed them into the congested hamper, which was in danger of exploding at any minute. As he moved to the steps, intending to fix himself another snack, Eden hemmed loudly behind him. He turned back to face Eden, her glistening, naked body nestling under the covers of the bed.

"Where are you going?"

"Downstairs, to get something to eat. Sorry. Are you hungry, too?"

"No." She patted the space next to her.

Thiago was baffled but decided to play along. In his previous sexual encounters, there had never been a need to stick around after the deed. He didn't understand how Earth girls would be any different, but he thought it wouldn't hurt to humor the touchy-feely human.

He lifted the sheets and climbed into bed next to her, laying perfectly, awkwardly still. Eden lay her head on his warm chest. His heartbeat intensified under her weight. Thiago could feel his tough exterior begin to soften. Slowly and carefully, he slipped his hand around her neck and held her close to him. He began petting the side of her head, threading her coppery curls through the spaces between his fingers.

Within moments, the pair was fast asleep and snoring in each other's arms.

CHAPTER 12

"Are you sure you want to go through with this?"

Thiago clipped a pair of aviator sunglasses onto the bridge of his nose, shielding his eyes from the glaring rays of the sun. Eden stood opposite him, clad in an all-black jumpsuit. Her flattened curls peeked out the bottom of her full-head helmet, bunched to one side in a long, tight ponytail.

She craned her neck upward, gazing through the blue tinted visor of her helmet. Five heavy sacks of millie flour painted with bullseye targets hung from the branches of a strapping, leafless tree. Thiago moved behind the trunk and prepared to change the positions of the sacks. Eden grunted, wielding a powerful weapon on the ground next to her.

The steel rod glinted as it caught the sunlight. The top consisted of a foul metal ball fitted with serrated spikes and the thick, upturned ends of screws and bolts. As she raised it high above her head, her sore arm hurt from repeatedly lifting the weapon.

"I'm sure. Bring it on."

The sacks of flour began dropping sequentially at varying lengths, with Thiago orchestrating the flow from behind the tree. Eden swung forward, her arm burning with fatigue and the repeated exertion of force. She missed the sack to her left on her first try. Her blow fell flat on the target behind it. As she froze momentarily thinking about her failure, a sack in her blind spot swung directly at her.

The bag smacked Eden in the visor, knocking her backward and onto the ground.

"Do you still think the helmet was a bad idea?" said Thiago slyly, extending his hand.

"Gloating's unattractive," Eden snapped back. She accepted his hand, allowing him to help her off the ground. Dusting off the dirt from the legs of her jumpsuit, she removed her helmet and held it against her waist. "I think I may have bitten off more than I can chew. My legs are sore from running with you every morning this week. I've fallen on my ass more times than I can count. I feel like I've got the brittle bones of a 90-year-old. What was I thinking?"

"The 90-year-olds on this planet are at the height of their physical abilities. What other excuses do you have?"

"I know, I know," Eden said miserably. She looked around at the makeshift training arena Thiago had meticulously constructed over the past few days. "When I asked if we could do a little one-on-one training session, I was expecting a couple of punching bags. Maybe I could run through some tires while you cheered me on from the sidelines."

"Are you giving up so soon? I knew it would be difficult for you, but I thought you'd last a little longer."

"I didn't say I was giving up," Eden interjected with a raised eyebrow. Her face glowed with determination. "I just need a little break."

"Good," said Thiago, a knowing smile settling on his lips. He handed her a flask filled with water from a satchel strapped across his back.

"Thanks," said Eden as she start taking huge gulps of water. She tipped the container back and splashed the rest of the water over her sweaty face. "Did you go to a bounty hunter training academy? Where did you learn to do everything?"

"Most bounty hunters are self-trained. I hauled in my first captive when I was fifteen. I've grown accustomed to being alone all my life. I guess I figured it was always better to be safe than sorry. I observed and learned from watching others – how to swim and scale obstacles. I've never needed anyone else. Hercules was sufficient company. He's taught me more than anyone else could."

"I can believe that," said Eden. Her heart warmed at the glisten of affection in Thiago's eyes every time he mentioned the name of his beloved companion.

"You need to be vigilant. You can never be too prepared for whatever's out here. Even the most out-of-shape schmuck on this planet has twice the upper body strength than that of a 'fit' human."

"Does this mean you're going to let me tag along on your next mission?"

"No," said Thiago bluntly. He was unmoved by the disappointed expression on Eden's face. "Your training is in case you ever have to defend yourself in the spaceship. You'd be more of a burden than a help to me right now."

"Thanks for the vote of confidence," mumbled Eden. She glared at the sacks of flour hanging above her. They were all completely intact. "What am I doing wrong?"

"You need to adjust your stance," said Thiago, enclosing her in a half-embrace from behind. He placed his hands gently over her fingers, closing them properly around the weapon. He guided her hands forward in a straight, swinging motion. "Raise the windsor above your head and strike down for the most powerful strike. For you to hit the targets, it's important to be aware of the placement of the windsor's head at all times. Do you think you can try again?"

Eden exhaled deeply, nodding. Thiago went around the tree and picked up the loose ropes off the ground, looping them around his fingers. Eden pulled her helmet over her head, her breath fogging up the visor. As she counted down internally, she made a thumbs-up sign with her hand.

"Ready!"

The sacks began dropping, taunting her as they dangled in front of her. An uninhibited war cry sprang from her lips as she charged forward, the weapon raised high above her head. Her eyes were glued to the sacks like she was a hungry predator. In swift, hacking motions, the spikes of her windsor pierced through each and every one of her moving targets. Adrenaline sizzled through her veins as she jumped up the tree. The ridged soles of her boots locked into the trunk. She lifted off the ground for only a moment, yet it was enough to bludgeon the last bag of millie flour to oblivion.

Eden landed on the ground, gawking at the scene around here. Coffee-colored grains leaked out of perforated holes in the bags and covered the ground in pools. Deflated sacks lay in the dirt like they'd been vigorously trampled by a stampede of horses. Thiago emerged from behind the tree, pride bursting from a toothy grin on his face.

"Not bad for a beginner. I'm impressed."

"Not bad?" Eden repeated giddily, breaking out in a victory dance. "I was magnificent! I didn't know I could do that! What are we going to do next?"

"Don't you want to take a break? Maybe get some lunch?"

"No!" Eden's eyes darted around the clearing of the training arena. "Let's do one more thing, and then I promise we can break for food."

"Whatever you say. Your shooting skills need a lot of work," Thiago agreed. He looked back at Hercules, who was chasing a couple of avians around the parked spaceship. "I'll be right back. I need to pick up some practice targets and fix Hercules a meal."

Eden placed her helmet on the ground and slowly wandered off to a cliff at the edge of the clearing. She unzipped a few inches from her jumpsuit, fanning her hands and welcoming a fresh draft onto her body.

A sense of vertigo gripped her as she gazed at the breathtaking violet and marigold scheme of the Runic territory fringe. The landscape was free from the pollution and smog in the city. A body of sparkling, flawlessly cerulean water was in the center of the land, surrounded by purple rock formations the size of small hills. Beyond the dreamy landscape were additional mountains and cliffs similar to hers. Slanting her head to one side, she began to relax.

Eden thought she could see the distinctive facial features of her sister Janine carved into the natural creases and crags on the side of a distant mountain. Of course, it was only a trick of her mind. In fact, she couldn't even see the resemblance unless she had her head positioned at a particular angle. Still, Eden tilted her head to the right again, a sense of nostalgia compelling her to take one step forward.

Mesmerized by the rock formation, she didn't notice she had stepped over a broken line on the cliff's edge. The ground began shaking from her weight. By the time she realized the danger, it was too late. The floor crumbled under her feet. Her twisting stomach churned at the sudden plunge.

Eden's arms flapped forward, managing to grab the jagged edge of the cliff. She kicked her feet as they dangled underneath her uselessly. Her voice sounded strange to her ears as she screamed and the color drained from her face. Terrified, she glanced up at her reddened fingers and white knuckles.

"Help! Thiago! Hercules! Help!"

Her fingers began to slip.

"Anyone..."

CHAPTER 13

Eden's palms clung to the ragged edge of the cliff. She winced, rivulets of blood oozing from her palms and down her arms. Her feet swung helplessly underneath her. As she kicked out her legs in desperation, her loosened left boot wriggled completely off her body. She glanced down and immediately regretted her decision. The boot plummeted through the air, bouncing against the edge twice before disappearing in a bed of saw-toothed rock formations below.

"I'm slipping..."

"Take my hand!" The delicately feminine hand of a woman appeared in front of Eden. Ornate rings studded with glowing moonstones and the planet's precious rocks embellished the stranger's fingers. The subtle gray tone to the woman's flesh was nearly translucent, displaying a network of veins under her skin.

The particulars of the hand flew right past Eden, who was overjoyed to see any assistance. Without a second to waste, she reached for the woman's fingers, her frantic cries slowly fading. The hand yanked her up the edge like a rag doll until she crashed onto the solid ground. She scuttled backward urgently, pushing with the raw palms of her hands.

"I'm alive," said Eden, cackling manically. She patted herself down, staining her jumpsuit with faint smears of blood. "I'm okay."

"Your hands are a bit scratched, and you're missing a shoe, but you'll be fine."

Eden's eyes focused on her savior. She pushed herself off the ground, splaying her arms to ward off her double vision. With her hand clutched over her heart surging with emotion and gratitude, she gushed, "I don't know how I can begin to thank you. I'm grateful you came along. I didn't think it would be right to die out here in this dirty place. I don't even like hiking."

"Slow down. You're still a little rattled. It's understandable, of course," said the stranger lightly. Her tinkling chuckle was pleasant to Eden's ears. "I think anyone would have done the same thing if they were in my position."

Eden wasn't sure if it was the close call or if she was simply under the influence of post-trauma hero worship. As she gazed up at her savior, who was at least 6 feet in height, there appeared to be a soft, golden radiance around the alien woman's figure.

The stranger had humanoid features, apart from the glittery gray of her thin skin, and she reminded Eden of a glamorous mermaid. Her glossy, light pink hair ran straight down her shoulders, stopping around her waist. Additionally, her savior was drop-dead gorgeous. The alien woman was aware of her beauty, flaunting her generous curves in a skintight jumpsuit with a narrow neckline that plunged down her stomach, revealing hints of her buxom chest.

"On this planet? I highly doubt that," said Eden darkly. She blinked, squinting her eyes at the familiar marking on the woman's forehead. Her eyes widened in realization. She had seen the same set of twin northbound arrows on Thiago.

Eden quickly concealed her inquisitive gaze, stepping forward with a sheepish smile and outstretched hand. "I'm sorry, I've been rude. I never had my life saved before, so I'm unfamiliar with the proper etiquette. My name's Eden."

The alien shook her hand and opened her mouth to speak. Before she could say anything, Thiago's gravelly voice came rumbling from behind them.

"Arleda!"

Both women turned to see Thiago jogging towards them and Hercules loping alongside him. The woman's peach-stained lips stretched out into a broad grin. She smoothed a lock of hair over her shoulders, waving animatedly at the approaching pair. Thiago dropped his bulky satchel onto the ground next to him. He frowned as his thick, blonde brows met in the middle of his forehead while he scanned the woman up and down.

"Thiago," the woman replied. She jutted out one foot and playfully placed a hand on her hip. "Well, look at you. You're even easier on the eyes than before."

"I look the same," said Thiago evenly. He made a face like someone had just shoved a can of tuna under his nose without warning. "What are you doing here? Eden, what happened to you? I only left you for a few minutes."

He looked back at Eden, whose unruly tangles of ginger hair looked even wilder than usual. They stuck to her sweaty cheeks in clumps, which were flushed red and scuffed with dirt. A filthy sock with a loosened garter was all that remained from her left boot. When his eyes landed on her swollen fingers, he saw open gashes speckling her knuckles and palms. Thiago dropped the amused smile from his face.

"Are you okay?" Thiago asked. He grabbed Eden's wrists to examine her cuts. "What happened?"

"It looks a lot worse than it is. I might feel it later," said Eden. Her shoulders shrank forward as she confessed. "I fell, and Arleda here showed up just in time and pulled me to safety. You could stand to be more polite to the woman who saved my life."

"The girl makes a lot of sense," Arleda piped up, cocking a pink eyebrow.

"Fell where?" said Thiago, ignoring the woman's remarks. He reached into one of the many pockets in his satchel and produced a large tube of salve.

Eden gagged as he unscrewed the cap, releasing a stench that smelled like a mixture of excrement and gym socks. Thiago squeezed out a coin-sized dollop and began applying it to Eden's cuts. She sucked in her teeth sharply at the burning sensation. Her breath slowly returned to normal as the burn turned into coldness.

"I was by the cliff," Eden answered as she massaged her wrists. She motioned toward the edge where she'd fallen. "It serves me right for trying to appreciate nature. In hindsight, it was probably a dumb idea to wander close to an edge without a fence or rail. I don't know how long I was screaming before Arleda showed up."

"Arleda saved you out of the goodness of her heart, huh?" said Thiago bluntly. He took a long, hard look at Arleda as if he were trying to figure out her end game. "How many credits are we talking about here? What are you looking for?"

Arleda tossed her head back in laughter as she gave Thiago's arm a squeeze. "Oh Thi-ger, don't be silly. Let's not give your new friend any incorrect impressions."

The three jumped back in shock as Hercules lunged at Arleda. Thiago jammed his arm between the angry creature's snapping pincers. Eden sprang forward and wrapped her arms around one of Hercules' legs. Her attempt to hold him back failed when she started gasping in pain. She released Hercules as the creature's hair began to dig into her wounds.

"Come on, Hercules," said Arleda, the smile on her face fading. She took a few steps back, raising a hand slowly. "You remember me, don't you, boy?"

"Hercules, heel," Thiago commanded, clicking his tongue comfortingly. He wiped the slime of his pet's drool on the side of his pants, his face scrunching up in disgust. "Damn it, Herc. Look at this mess. "

"I don't know why Herc is misbehaving. I've never seen him randomly attack like that," noted Eden aloud. Feeling the heat of Arleda's gaze, she added helpfully, "My sister and I used to have an iguana when we were kids. They shed a lot when they're growing, and they can get cranky. Maybe that's why old Herc is upset." She paused. "I don't know what I'm saying."

"You could be right," said Arleda, the sweet smile on her face making a reappearance. "That's okay. I'm sure Hercules didn't mean it. You're sorry, aren't you, boy?"

"Maybe it's the vile boisenflower perfume you insist on swimming in every morning," said Thiago. He unpacked a small container from his satchel and opened it, flinging a slab of meat into the distance. The creature instantly perked up, nearly sliding off-balance on its eight feet before chasing after the treat.

Arleda stuck her tongue out. She gestured with her thumb and pointer finger, the local equivalent of flipping the bird at Thiago.

Eden wasn't sure why, but she felt a brush of jealousy at the history between the two. She cleared her throat as she drummed her fingertips against each other. Trying her best to portray careless nonchalance, she commented, "You two seem to know each other well."

Arleda batted her long lashes as she winked in Thiago's direction. "We're well-acquainted, aren't we, Thiago?"

"She dabbles in bounty hunting too. We used to do missions together and split the reward," he explained.

"I'd say I did more than that. Admit it, we made a pretty good team, didn't we?" Arleda insisted. She peeked at Eden, crinkling her nose. "Of course, that was quite some time ago."

"You weren't half bad," said Thiago flatly.

He placed two looped fingers in his mouth and whistled for Hercules. The creature trotted back to his owner, licking off the blood from its mouth. "I guess we should pack up and hit the road. I assume you've completed training for the day?"

"Yeah," said Eden, nodding fervently. "I think I've achieved my adrenaline fix, thank you very much. Arleda, is your ship close by?"

"Are you still driving around that hoverbike?" asked Thiago, peering around at his surroundings.

Eden couldn't believe it. Not only was Arleda built like a voluptuous comic book heroine, she apparently kicked ass like one, too. She imagined Arleda on a glinting speedster bike, gliding through a backdrop of heavenly skies as her perfect hair whipped back in the wind.

"I finally decided to sell my old girl," said Arleda, unfurling her bottom lip. She sighed for effect. "I made sure to find her a good home. I have a ship of my own now. It had been acting up much more recently, so I decided to take it to the repair shop at Runic Central, but of course, with my luck, it broke down. Now it's completely dead. I've tried everything, but that thing isn't budging."

"Oh no," said Eden. "Where did it break down?"

"Not too far from here. I was out here looking for help when I found you."

"I can head back to my ship and call a towing company."

"You could also hitch a ride with us," Eden blurted. Her heart raced, and she couldn't shake the feeling that she might be inviting trouble. But Arleda saved her life, and Eden felt grateful. She didn't want to leave Arleda stranded. Besides, Thiago and Eden's exclusivity was only sanctified through a shady intergalactic operation involving TerraMates and an underground auction house.

Wasn't it?

"I don't know if that's such a good idea," Thiago muttered, scratching the back of his head.

"That's very kind of you to offer, Eden," said Arleda. Something about the tone of her voice told Eden she wasn't entirely sincere. "I don't want to put anyone out."

"All right, then don't."

"You won't be!" Eden reassured her, shooting Thiago a deathly glare. She spoke through gritted teeth. "What Thiago meant to say was, we would be glad to tow your ship. It's the least we can do."

"It's the least you can do," Thiago pointed out, staring blankly at Eden. Noting the vein bulging out of Eden's temple, he swiftly changed his tune. "Sure. Whatever!

Show me your ship, and we'll get it hooked onto the back of mine. "

"Wonderful! I think I've got an inflatable hovering pad lying around somewhere," said Arleda gleefully. She turned to Thiago, smiling brightly. "Oh Thi-ger, I'll need your help fastening my craft to yours."

"Lead the way. I'll be right behind you."

"Don't keep her waiting, Thi-ger," Eden grumbled under her breath. She bitterly crushed a piece of gravel under her remaining boot.

"What was that?"

"I didn't say anything," Eden said innocently, her cheeks blushing furiously. "I'll get myself washed up. Herc and I will meet you guys back at your ship. "

"Right. We won't be long," said Thiago slowly. As he walked away from her, there was an inkling of a smile lingering on his lips.

"Come on, Hercules, let's go. I need a shower to wash off this stink," said Eden as Hercules settled next to her. She stroked the top of his furry head as the creature nuzzled lovingly against her side. "What were you thinking, scaring Arleda like that? That wasn't very nice of you."

Hercules blubbered in resentment as if to defend himself.

"Whatever you say, Mr. Grumpy," said Eden sternly. She nudged him with her knee, easing the creature off the ground. "Come on now, let's get out of here."

Eden paused, catching a glimpse of Arleda and Thiago out of the corner of her eye. She watched a giggling Arleda touch Thiago gently on the arm. The distance between the pair was steadily shrinking. A twist of dread brewed in the pit of her stomach. Eden averted her spying eyes and began moving back to Thiago's spaceship.

Perhaps asking Thiago's ex-flame to tag along wasn't a great idea after all.

CHAPTER 14

"Your ship hasn't changed at all since the last time I was here, and that was almost two years ago," Arleda mused, stroking her chin. "Would you like me to set you up with an interior designer? You can have Jacqua's information. The man is a miracle. He'll know what to do to fix this place up."

"I'm not interested, but thanks," said Thiago from the passenger's seat.

He pulled back the green lever next to his steering controls. Mirrors from either side of the ship disengaged, mechanically setting themselves into position. He peered into each mirror, wanting to make sure Arleda's luxurious ship was still firmly attached to the hover pad latched to the back of his spaceship. Hearing the familiar sound of Arleda bustling about behind him as she loudly began to rearrange his furniture, his grip tightened on the wheel.

"Arleda," said Thiago loudly, hoping to distract her. He checked out Arleda's ship through the mirrors again. It was a luxurious triple-decker vessel with top-of-the-line lights and shields with sleek stripes the color of ruby and onyx. The ship had weapons, too; there was a large turret on the roof and four archer missile launchers fused to the sides. It was a terrifying combination of violence and femininity. "That ship of yours is quite the looker. How much did she cost?"

"Isn't it grand?" Arleda agreed, beaming in admiration. "You better be extra careful with her. That's my baby you've got back there! It didn't come cheap, but I finally decided something. After all these years on the road, I wasted too much time breaking my back and eliminating one bad guy at a time. I'd never taken any time to do anything for myself, so I decided I deserved a treat."

Thiago snickered but instantly clammed up and looked behind himself when Arleda fell silent. She narrowed her eyes in Thiago's direction. The tiny diamond hoop around her left nostril jiggled as they flared.

"Do you find something funny, Thiago?"

"Not at all," said Thiago. His face lost all emotion as he nodded at her to continue. "Sorry. What were you were saying?"

"I decided to splurge. It put a five million credit hole in my pocket, but it is well worth it if you ask me."

"Five million what?" Thiago repeated. He was flabbergasted. Thiago's eyes flashed as he turned to question her. "Are you talking about a different type of credit?"

"Full-fledged, intergalactically accepted credits. Of course!" replied Arleda without missing a beat.

"Well then – in that case, good for you."

Thiago turned back to face the windshield. He kept his eyes straight in front of him as the spaceship glided through the clouds and burnt sienna haze of the sunset.

Although he tried not to show any emotion, something didn't feel right. Warning bells were ringing in his head.

He had only been with Arleda for a short time, but for the six months they decided to join forces and work together, he'd gotten a taste of Arleda's deep-seated gambling addiction. Although he'd caught onto her vice soon after their partnership began, he initially refrained from interfering because she was a terrific fighter.

Like Thiago, she had grown up without her parents. The difference between the two was that she had no recollection of them at all. After she bounced around from one foster home to another, each with living conditions and harsh environments more deplorable than the next, she finally ended up on the streets.

A Thymore alien named Demitri took Arleda under his wing when she was twelve years old. A disgraced monk from one of the most famous monasteries on the planet, Demitri banded a group of homeless street urchins together into an organized gang. The children scoured shops and broke into residences for food and valuables under their leader's direction. The group stayed together for years until Demitri's sudden and unexplained disappearance.

With no manipulative glue to hold the children together, they disbanded. At the time, Arleda was seventeen. Armed with years of monastic martial arts training and street smarts honed to near-perfection, she set out to take on the world by herself.

Arleda had some of the quickest reflexes Thiago had ever seen. She had pinned him down on multiple occasions when they regularly trained together. But when Arleda began showing up late to their missions from late-night card games at underground casinos, half-awake and grumpy from another substantial loss, Thiago grew weary of her. When she failed up to show up for the third mission in a row, and he found her barely lucid and immersed in an all-night card game, it was enough for him.

He made the logical decision of cutting ties with her before she could drag him down. He hadn't thought about her since then, but as Arleda had mentioned, nearly two years had passed. Thiago wanted to keep things civil with Arleda for the sake of Eden. He should make an effort to give her the benefit of the doubt. Two years were long enough for people to change. Maybe Arleda truly had a change of heart, and she was prepared to leave the past behind her.

Arleda lifted her nose in the air, sniffing defensively. "I don't think I like the accusatory tone in your voice. Am I detecting a hint of jealousy?"

"There's no tone, Arleda. I don't know what you mean."

"If you must know, our break-up turned out to be the best thing that's ever happened to me. For one thing, I'm getting a hundred percent of my bounty rewards." She signed. "I tried to be classy and raise myself above petty bickering, but you know what I think?"

"I most certainly do not. Do I look like a mind reader to you?"

"I think it bothers you to see me succeed."

"Don't be ridiculous, Arleda. You're welcome to think what you'd like, but I'm genuinely happy to see you back on your feet again."

"Oh, Thi-ger," Arleda drawled. She slunk up to him, walking her fingers along the curves of his ear. Thiago's shoulders stiffened as he felt the contours of her breasts gently pressed against his back. He leaned away from her as she continued. "You know, I could always tell when you're lying."

"What's going on, guys?"

Eden strolled through the doorway of the cockpit as she wrung out her muted copper hair with a towel. Feeling refreshed after a much-needed shower, she had dumped her shredded clothes, and currently wore a crisp tangerine jumpsuit. Thiago's eyes darted to the indoor mirror Eden had installed a few days ago, settling on her reflection. He observed a drop in Eden's jumpsuit zipper, revealing a dimple of her cleavage. He smiled to himself as his eyes moving back to the windshield.

"I'm sorry," said Eden. Her voice was slightly shaky. "Am I interrupting something?"

"Oh, no," said Arleda, her full, pearly-white grin returning. She sauntered away from Thiago's side. "We were merely reminiscing, weren't we, Thiago?"

"Whatever you say."

"Sounds like fun," said Eden. She gave up her attempt to keep the towel knotted in place around her head and sighed. "I wish you had something to dry my hair around here. Are you hungry? I was on my way to put something in the oven to eat."

"Not me, thanks. But what's that I hear? Thiago, have you been forcing Eden to live with your grotesque man-products? You poor thing," said Arleda, holding a hand to her chest sympathetically. She strode over to a chrome trunk she had brought on board.

Arleda popped it open. A soft whirring sound emitted from the container as three tiers rose to the top. Eden's eyes lit up. Arleda had packed it with an incredible selection of neatly presented beauty products. Sparkling compact powders and eyeshadow palettes swirled in beautiful containers.

"That looks fantastic," breathed Eden. Her mouth watered at what looked like an entire cosmic Sephora aisle sitting inside the trunk.

"Doesn't it?" said Arleda proudly. She studied Eden's shoes and began shaking her head in pity. "Oh honey, don't tell me, let me guess. Thiago did the shoe shopping for you, didn't he? The only time a woman would ever choose buckles that size and in those awful color would be at gunpoint. Let me see if I can find something in here for you."

"It's okay. These shoes aren't runway-worthy, but they are pretty comfortable. I'm not sure we're the same size."

"Please. You're not on Earth any longer. My feet are sensitive to anything other than the most fashionable designer smart shoes available in the galaxy. All my shoes and clothes adjust to the wearer's proportions."

Before Eden could politely decline again, Arleda stooped down and began rifling through the bottom level of the trunk. Eden gasped as Arleda pulled out and displayed a series of trendsetting shoes that would put all the Kardashian sisters to shame. The bold designs and vibrant splashes of color were nothing like Eden had ever seen back on Earth. They ranged from boots to platforms to double and triple-wedged heels with all sorts of complicated knots, unnecessary zippers, and shoe beds that made you stand at unexpected angles. Eden's eyes remained fixed on a pair of gladiator-like heels with crisscrossing beige straps running up to the knees. Its heels were thick, transparent wedges filled with neon-colored tadpoles swimming in pink-tinted water.

Arleda watched Eden devour the shoes with her eyes. She smiled, scooping up the gladiator heels and handing them over to Eden. "Go ahead. Try them on."

"I don't know if I should."

"Don't be shy," Arleda urged encouragingly. Her eyes brightened with an idea that cropped up in her mind. She turned over to the driver's seat, calling out to Thiago. "Why don't we make a quick pit stop at the Odi

Pauperum Lounge? We'll all get some dinner and get to know each other some more. It will be my treat!"

"That sounds fancy," said Eden, who was only half-listening as she admired her shoes. She had slipped into the gladiator heels, which perfectly molded to the shape of her feet.

"It's beautiful! I'm sure Thiago doesn't bring you out much. It's a pity."

"You're talking about one of the most expensive parts of Runic Territory," said Thiago solemnly, keeping his eyes focused outside. "Security there is airtight. How would you expect Eden to get around?"

"Have you forgotten that I have the best prosthetics and make-up products in the galaxy?" said Arleda confidently, her mind clearly set on the idea. "Come on Thiago, it will be just like we used to do an operation when we went undercover."

"That was different. We were working. The lounge could be dangerous for Eden."

"It will be just like the old days. Don't be that way, Thiago," Arleda pleaded. She looked at Eden meaningfully for support.

"Don't we have to eat?" said Eden, smiling. She was becoming increasingly stir-crazy and was dying to get out of Thiago's spaceship. "I know the rules. I won't draw any attention to myself. You'll be there the whole time!"

"I, on the other hand, have a plan for Eden's new look," said Arleda, rubbing her hands. She winked at Eden. "I've got a whole wardrobe of clothes back on my ship. So many, in fact, I still haven't gotten around to wearing them all. You are in excellent hands."

Thiago frowned as he thought about his situation. He could hear a quiver of eager anticipation in Eden's voice, and he couldn't bring himself to be the one to extinguish her dreams. He looked back to see Eden and Arleda hunched towards each other, talking and giggling behind him inaudibly.

To his surprise, Arleda seemed to be genuinely attempting not only civility but generosity towards Eden. Eden wasn't just any woman – she was a human woman. Two years ago, he would have laughed himself silly if someone had suggested Arleda was capable of conversing with an alien. Today, here he was, witnessing it with his eyes.

"I suppose we can stop by at that lounge. Two hours at most, then we have to leave."

His chest warmed at the sound of Eden's gleeful squeals. Arleda whisked her away and out of the cockpit, activating the drone features of the trunk with a remote control. The trunk ascended from the floor, slowly following them.

Thiago pursed his lips thoughtfully as he set course for the restaurant. Perhaps it wouldn't hurt to let his guard down a little around Arleda. She was his former partner, after all. Perhaps she had changed for the better.

CHAPTER 15

"Are we ready to leave yet?"

Thiago slid down the couch, groaning miserably. He had been alone for too long and forgotten how long it took one woman to get ready to go out, let alone two. He managed to stop the impatient tapping of his boot against the floor and rose from his seat, shuffling into the kitchen. Smoothing the length of white-blonde hair he had neatly slicked back for the occasion, he examined his reflection on the reflective surface of the overhanging cupboard.

He had never been the type to loiter in front of mirrors. Now that he found himself looking at his face, he couldn't deny the real change in his appearance since Eden's arrival. Perhaps the 'cuddling' thing Eden insisted on after love-making had affected him more than he cared to admit. The saggy bags under his eyes were less prominent than before.

The acute bouts of pain that plagued his limbs from overzealous physical exertion on his missions still bothered him daily. Instead of being left to toss and turn on his spacious old bed in complete solitude, which typically woke him up multiple times in a single night, he found himself sleeping better than ever. Something about Eden's presence assured him a night of satisfying sleep, not unlike that of a hibernating Hercules with a store of food in his belly big enough to render him immovable through winter.

Thiago flattened the creases on the overlapping dark denim lapels of his coat. The leather sleeves of his rarely used formal wear breathed lightly with each of his movements.

He examined a square steel band around his wrist. He had bolted the center himself with a single piece of burnt screw found in the remains of his father's workshop. He pressed down on the button, making ghostly green digits project onto his arm.

"*Come on*, Arleda, Eden. You said we were going to leave in five minutes. That was half an hour ago."

Thiago spun around at the noise of the bathroom door opening. Arleda paraded into the room. Half of her pushed-up breasts poured out of a tiny strapless dress miraculously clinging to her body. She twirled around, showing off dizzying intricate patterns on her gaudy golden dress and a peek of her butt.

"Do you like it?"

He blinked, averting his eyes from her open invitation. Thiago managed to focus his attention on her hair instead, which Arleda had intricately coiled around her head like a nest of pink snakes.

"You look lovely," said Thiago tonelessly. He stretched out his neck, his eyes gliding right past Arleda's shoulder. "Now where's Eden?" Thiago gulped, feeling his words trail off at the abrupt knotting in his chest.

Eden wrapped a hand around the side of the doorway. Her intent was to guide herself out of the bathroom, but the result was making her concealed body more alluring for Thiago. She wore one of Arleda's silver couture dresses, with large clusters of looped wiring and pinpoints of small lights for a collar. Biting down on her lip, Eden did a tentative twirl as Arleda peppered her with poise and make-up retention tips from the side.

Thiago had only ever seen Eden's hair in its all-natural, frizzy state. Although he possessed an unspoken love for her curls, her glamorous appearance stunned him speechless. She had completely straightened her fiery curls and gathered back her hair in a long ponytail wrapped with silver spirals. The hair pushed away from her face revealed pointed, elfin ear prosthetics. Geometric triangles of the Jadene alien race lined her cheeks. His eyes skimmed her long, graceful legs, her lanky frame appearing taller with the gladiator heels.

"Didn't I tell you I was a miracle worker? I could turn a Blazian's ear into a silk purse," said Arleda cheerfully, arranging the billowy skirt wiring under the corset of Eden's dress. She glanced up at Eden with an apologetic smile, quickly adding, "Not that I'm making any comparisons, of course."

"I'm going to be the first one to say it. I feel and look ridiculous," said Eden, turning to head back into the bathroom. "I should change into something else."

"Don't! You look great!" said Thiago. He hemmed, looking away as he scratched at a nonexistent itch on the back of his sweaty neck. "What I meant was, you look presentable."

"Really?" said Eden, cracking a smile.

"Look at the time. Thiago's right," said Arleda suddenly, a cheery smile plastered on her face. She ushered Eden toward the front door. "We should get going before they cancel our reservations."

"This lounge is out of this world," said Eden with delight as she shoveled a forkful of fruit salad into her mouth. She washed down the salad with a glass of flower-scented water. Her grip tightened around the stem of her gold-stained wineglass as she quickly added, "I suppose it's only out of my world."

In spite of Arleda's best attempts to give the trio a makeover, the group still managed to stand out from the Runic patrons of the restaurant. The shortest of the three, Eden, still towered over the average Runic's four-foot height. They were tucked away in one of the isolated corner booths in the back. Eden had to keep herself from rudely ogling the Runics. They reminded her of smooth-skinned goblins dressed in their Sunday best. They had webbed hands and feet; their rough skin was the color and texture of tar.

"I'm pleased to see you are enjoying yourself," said Arleda, raising her glass for a toast. She swirled around a rich plum liquid in her glass while she unfolded her bottom lip. "It's a shame you can't have any of the

Bambina wine. The taste is simply sublime. Sadly, almost all alcohol on HT-007 is toxic to humans."

"Keep your voice down," said Thiago sternly, an eyebrow shooting up disdainfully. "You should know better than to broadcast your secrets all over a bar."

"Will you relax?" said Arleda, shaking her head. She raked her hand playfully across the length of Thiago's arm. "You were always wound too tightly."

"I spotted one of Malatov's direct subordinates in one of the private rooms. You don't want to risk having your lounge membership revoked, do you?"

"We're in a private booth of our own," Arleda responded in defense. The hoop around her nostril bobbed as she spoke. "Why do you always have to second-guess me?"

Eden remained blissfully unaware of the bickering between her companions. "Have you tasted this, Arleda?" Eden asked innocently. She deliberately sliced off a chunk of the torc tenderloin on her plate, causing a river of juices and blood to trickle out from the meat. "This cut is delicious. Thank you so much for taking us out to dinner."

"It wasn't a problem at all," said Arleda. She softened immediately as soon as Eden started stroking her ego. "Thiago, I understand your next target is a Runic native. I suppose that nasty bastard Salabar is next on your agenda?"

"As a matter of fact, he is," said Thiago, nodding his head as he crunched down on a piece bread. "I can't wait to get my hands on that filthy scum."

"That sounds dangerous," said Eden, shifting uneasily in her seat. "What's his story?"

"He's another traitor who willingly fed secrets of his species to Malatov and the Noxx army," said Thiago, gesturing with his half-eaten bread still in hand. "He's wanted for running one of the largest networks of trafficking and prostitution on the planet. Don't let his diminutive stature fool you. People think he committed crimes in over one hundred fifty different territories."

"I'm impressed you've managed to track him down," said Arleda, her intelligent eyes narrowing. "Do you remember when we took down his partner, Drako? The one with the undercover brothel scheme? Drako tried to jump out the window when we revealed ourselves to him."

"He ended up falling into a vat of discarded lard and grease the kitchen left sitting out in the back," said Thiago, chuckling.

"You know, we did make a solid team at some point. We caught Drako together. What do you think about teaming up for old time's sake and taking down Salabar?"

"That doesn't sound like a great idea, to be honest."

"There you go again, being your negative nebula self," said Arleda. She turned to Eden. "Why don't we ask her what she thinks?"

"Huh? Sure. I mean, yes, whatever you said sounds like a good idea." Eden smiled vaguely. She hadn't heard a word of the conversation, actively tuning it out to enjoy the meal. As Arleda continued to work on changing Thiago's mind, Eden's eyes drifted to the opening of the private room across from their booth.

The paper sliding door stood slightly ajar, revealing the brightly-lit interior of the room. Below a ceiling decorated with floating paper lanterns set against a romantic projection of a starry night, Eden watched a disturbing scene.

The elderly Noxx official Thiago saw earlier now occupied the end of a long, empty table draped with an antique white tablecloth and lace place settings. Next to him was a young human woman clad in a spellbinding floor-length gown. Her corset bodice was a gorgeous, regal blue and inlaid with honey-gold designs and trimmings. Although her jewelry was flashy and the makeup on her face looked perfect, there was not a breath of life in her glassy hazel eyes. Eden saw the reason for her docility around the woman's neck. She wore an ominous shock collar encrusted with diamonds and colorful stones, the beauty of the gemstones masking the danger of the necklace.

Eden watched hesitantly as the Noxx held up a spoonful of thick, foul-looking soup to the woman's mouth. She turned away from him, leaning back in her chair as her face grimaced in revulsion. The Noxx sneered, revealing a set of bleeding gums. The mottled feathers that crowned his head spread forward as he calmly sat back in his chair with his spoon still raised in the air. He reached for a small remote on the table to his side and pressed down on the button as a sickening smile spread on his lips.

A sudden flurry of sparks lit up on the woman's collar, sending her convulsing and lurching forward in pain.

"Oh no!" yelled Eden. Her cheeks flushed red from the sudden attention Thiago and Arleda diverted towards her. Eden flashed them a guilty smile. "Sorry. I thought I saw a rat run across the floor. False alarm."

Eden peeked back into the room. The woman's shoulders were slumped forward in defeat, obediently lapping the contents of the spoon held in front of her. Eden's heart pounded against her chest. She cut herself another slice of her steak, crossing her legs to conceal the moist spot growing between her legs.

"Can I help you with something?" asked Thiago, shrugging off his formal wear with the speed and angst of a teenager who had been forced to dress up for a fancy dinner party.

Eden was hunched over in his open closet, rummaging through unfolded heaps of clothing on his floor like a forgetful squirrel searching for a buried acorn.

"Where did you put the shock collar you found with me?" asked Eden, resting her chin on her shoulder. "You didn't throw it away, did you?"

"No, you never know when you'll need something like that," said Thiago slowly. Those were the last words he had expected to come out of her mouth. And she had mentioned it offhandedly, as well. "Why would you be looking for such a thing?"

"Trust me," said Eden, rising off the ground.

She shimmied out of Arleda's dress and laid it on the side of a chair. Gently removing the spirals holding her sleek ponytail in place, she lay the slinky hair accessory on the nightstand. His enchanted eyes watched as her loosened hair fell around her shoulders, a few tousled strands sexily framing her face.

"So where is it?"

Thiago opened the third drawer of the nightstand and felt around the bottom, retrieving an ugly collar along with a remote control. Eden took the collar from him and fastened it around her neck. She closed her palm over the control in his hands, a wicked smile crossing her lips as she gazed up at him.

"Could you hold onto this for me?"

Before Thiago could ask any questions, Eden flung her arms around him. She pulled him close hungrily, keeping him silent as she kissed him with the all the passion she had pent up from the restaurant. Something about the morally reprehensible, yet titillating scene she witnessed aroused something she never knew existed inside her.

There was nothing more she wanted at that moment than to let Thiago have his way with her. The intense satisfaction that sparked in Thiago's eyes as he controlled his last target, Krypt, with his mind-control theremin device, made Eden yearn for a similar sensation.

Eden broke away from the sloppy kiss. She fell back on the bed, daintily wiping the sides of her mouth with the back of her hand. With a mischievous grin on her face, Eden slipped off her panties and tossed them aside. She spread her legs wide open to taunt him, stroking her drenched folds with the tips of her fingers. A whispered moan came out of her lips as her middle finger squeezed her sex. She thrust the finger in and out of her quivering folds, her fluttering eyes locking onto Thiago's.

"Don't just stand there. What are you waiting for?" Eden teased him through clenched teeth. "Go ahead. Zap me."

"What?"

"Do it, Thiago. Trust me."

His finger hovered tentatively over the button of the control, his Adam's apple bobbing as he stared at her. The hardening bulge in his pants swelled with every pumping movement of her nimble finger. Lost in the euphoria present on her beautifully contorting face, he gently pressed down on the control.

A momentary spark shot off once on her shock collar. Eden gasped, her eyelids snapping back. She purred faintly, her lowering head sinking back into his pillows.

"Again."

Thiago obliged. He tentatively held the button down for three seconds before his finger bounced off the knob. The bulge between his legs throbbed at the sight her jiggling breasts, trembling along with the short, sensual spasms of her body. Stumbling out of his underwear, he climbed onto the bed. He moved on top of her, his cock dragging against her calf and up the warm flesh of her thighs.

Eden clutched a clump of his hair in her fist, licking a trail along his musky neck as she whispered into his ear.

"Don't hold back."

CHAPTER 16

"I bring bad news, kids."

Arleda sauntered out from the central office of the spacecraft repair station. The station was enormous, claiming a commercial-sized pod for itself, and hovered over thirty thousand feet above ground level. She crossed the landing strip toward Eden and Thiago, who were playing fetch with Hercules by Thiago's parked spaceship.

"I just spoke to five different employees at the station," Arleda announced as she approached them. She crossed her arms, sighing theatrically. "The flight software on my craft is too advanced for these Runic hicks. It's not just that they don't have my processor in stock. They don't even carry the one I need! Can you believe it?"

"That's what I tried to explain to you back on my ship," said Thiago. He snorted unpleasantly. "If you would have listened to me, we could have avoided this waste of time."

"Be nice," Eden whispered. She could already feel the slow creep of Arleda's stay extending past the Salabar mission. Turning to Arleda, she chimed in helpfully. "I'm sorry their customer service wasn't more helpful. Did they recommend a shop that carries what you need?"

"As a matter of fact, they did," said Arleda crossly, tapping a finger against her cheek in thought. "It's in a station all the way out on the border between the Glop and Curvehorn territories. I couldn't ask you to take me all the way there. It would be too much of a burden."

"Great. I was afraid you were going to ask us for another ride."

Eden prodded Thiago's side, inadvertently striking him square in the ribs. She saw how Arleda's prissy tendencies could irritate anyone. However, she couldn't understand what triggered Thiago's animosity toward an ex-partner that used to help him bring in a lot of money. In fact, Thiago had never mentioned Arleda before.

Of course, Eden wasn't naive. She knew there had been more to Arleda and Thiago's partnership than what she saw on the surface. Still, Eden prided herself on being trustworthy. The promise she made to Arleda involved completion of her ship repairs, and Eden was going to deliver if it was possible.

"It wouldn't be any burden at all. We can have a look right after you send Salabar to the authorities."

"Eden, if only all Earthlings were as sweet and considerate as you," Arleda bubbled, wrapping her arm around Eden in a tight squeeze. She paused for effect. "Or had half your smarts. You don't seem the self-important, educated type. Maybe the humans wouldn't be miserable on this planet."

Arleda's candid tone sounded as innocent as ever. The brutal and ignorant remark caught Eden off guard. She frowned. Was it possible that she was reading too much between lines that only existed in her mind? She looked over at Thiago to see if he had overheard the conversation. Apparently he had not. He was busy rubbing the top of Hercules' head, praising the creature for his skill at retrieving objects.

"Um, I don't think..."

"Oh dear, will you look at how late it's getting? I'll have to ask one of the station boys to keep my ship in storage while we take down Salabar. Let's hope they've got enough sense to keep my baby intact while I'm away, or I'll be forced to sue," Arleda spoke to herself breezily, peering up at the darkening skies overhead. "It looks like a storm's about to break over the horizon, too. Come on, let's not waste time. We've got a criminal overlord to catch."

Thiago whistled and pulled a stuffed bone away from Hercules' slobbering mouth. The creature ran and scuttled behind his master, boarding the cargo door of the spaceship. Arleda marched back into the station, her shrill demands audible to Eden through the closed doors.

Eden blew a disgruntled raspberry at Arleda through her lips. She headed towards Thiago's ship as well, dragging her feet underneath her.

The wheels of Thiago's ship touched down soundlessly on a plot of land in the jungle surrounding Runic territory. Eden pressed her nose against the glass of her passenger window, inspecting her surroundings with bewildered fascination. Giant trees with lopsided trunks the height and width of Earth-sized industrial trucks jutted out from the land, disturbing the flat area around the clearing. The sticky leaves of trees stayed together naturally, forming long, swooping curls that looked like the limp crown of a jester's hat. Two-toned tulips budded out from the ends of leaves like little rusty bells.

Thiago unbuckled his restraint, rising from the pilot's seat. "Okay, Eden, you'll have to wait here. Remember to keep the shields active this time. There's some leftover salad and honeyberry macaroons in the fridge if you get hungry."

"You can trust me. And I'm incredibly grateful for Arleda's portable television," added Eden, waving a twelve-inch flatscreen device in the air victoriously. "I guess it would be unrealistic to receive Earth broadcasts out here, but I'll make do. Stay safe, you guys. I, on the other hand, will sit back, relax, and watch whatever I can with a glass of bubbly by my side. And by bubbly, I mean my favorite soda."

"You can go ahead and keep the television. I've got three spares back home," said Arleda as she strapped on a striking pair of red multi-functional boots. "Eden, how is your self-defense training going with Thiago? I hope his vicious temper and dated methods haven't kept you from learning how to beat up bad guys."

"It can get pretty strenuous sometimes," Eden admitted with a shrug. "I have to say, Thiago's an excellent teacher. I didn't start from much, but I think I'm improving."

"Is that so?" said Arleda as she removed her weapon satchel from the hooks on the cockpit wall. "Why don't you come with us tonight? You can shadow me and give your skills a live test."

"Not a chance," interjected Thiago. "Eden doesn't have enough experience to get out on the field, and she might hurt herself."

"Where is she going to acquire real-world experience, if not in a real situation?" challenged Arleda, folding her arms across her chest. "Don't tell me you're afraid of that little runt Salabar? We will both be there! It's the safest scenario for Eden. You don't think I'd let anything happen to her under my watch, do you?"

"Well, no, but it doesn't make sense to take unnecessary risks."

"Hey," Eden called out, exhaling in frustration as she turned to face them in her swiveling chair. "I'm right here."

"My apologies, Eden," said Arleda as she checked the contents of her satchel. "I just think hands-on experience is the best way to learn. I would be delighted to teach you everything I know."

"I find it incredible I need to repeat myself," Thiago rumbled, his voice thick with annoyance. "But Eden's simply not ready for it."

"You know what? I think I'd like to take Arleda up on her offer," said Eden churlishly. Her arched brows practically merged at the center of her displeased, wrinkled forehead. She was frustrated with Thiago. Eden didn't like it when anyone took it upon themselves to speak for her. She wouldn't have tolerated it back on Earth, and she wasn't about to start now in space.

"Don't underestimate the Runics, especially Salabar and his crew," Thiago insisted, scowling at Eden. "They may look small, but they're swift and much stronger than their size would indicate. We aren't even halfway through your training yet."

"I know, but I think Arleda's correct. I'll need to step out of my comfort zone at some point." She looked at Thiago pointedly. "Granted, I could do with a little more target practice, but I think I know how to swing a windsor now."

Thiago shook his head, pulling down a lever to activate the shields.

Nothing happened.

He pulled the lever again, hoping that the same action would have different results this time, and made an exasperated sound when the shields refused to deploy. Pulling up a control panel on the dashboard screen, he began a troubleshooting procedure. He tried repeatedly but couldn't get the shields down. All his attempts resulted in irritating sounds reinforcing failure after failure.

"Unbelievable. The shields are not functioning," Thiago muttered, nearly crushing the shield lever in a last futile attempt. "That's strange. They seemed to have been working last night when I tested them."

"You should have gotten your ship checked out back at the station like I recommended," Arleda sang. She lifted up one side of her mouth. The gold flakes crusted on her lips shimmered under the cockpit lighting. Her face turned solemn. "There are a few ancient Runic tribes scattered all over the area. They are uncivilized, violently unstable, and don't need provocation to attack. Leaving Eden here without any sort of protection on your spaceship would be just as irresponsible, if not more dangerous, than bringing her with us."

Eden imagined a horde of angry Runics with bloodied spears, blasters, and bags of explosives strapped over their knobby little shoulders. Shuddering at the thought of a hundred slimy webbed hands pawing at her as they pinned her down, she leaped to her feet. The imagery was frightening and perhaps the product of a disturbed imagination, but she wasn't going to take any chances.

"I'm convinced now. I'm not staying here."

"Fine. I guess we're all going then," Thiago conceded. He took a quick look at Eden's outfit. It was a pink jumpsuit she had borrowed from Arleda. "You may want to change into something more water-resistant."

As if on cue, a brief burst of blinding lightning flashed outside the spaceship windows, followed by the ground-quaking roar of thunder. Waves of rain began pattering noisily against the ship top and windshields, solidifying his case.

135

"Thiago's right," said Arleda, reaching into her satchel. She switched on a computer and headed out the door without consulting with anyone. "Let me see if I can get a head start. It's going to be difficult locating Salabar's cavern in this terrible weather. "

"Thanks. I'll round up Hercules."

"Thiago, wait," Eden called after him, hastily grabbing his arm.

"What is it?"

"I know you're worried," said Eden softly, squeezing his hand. "I'm scared, too. But I'll promise you something. I'm going to keep my mouth shut and my ears open. I'll listen to every word you say."

"You really want to tag along with me, don't you?"

"I do. I should probably contribute to society somehow, shouldn't I? Even if the people around me are aliens? If you're worried about splitting the bounty with me, don't be. I'm not interested in the money. Technically, we are married. Humans are barely people here, so you're morally obligated to make sure I don't die in your care."

"Equality laws don't apply to humans," said Thiago, laughing. "Okay. You've got five minutes to meet us in front."

"You know what? I'll be out in three. I promise I won't let you down."

"Good. I know you won't."

CHAPTER 17

Eden shivered, sniffling her wrinkled nose as the pouring rain attacked her like a runaway shower head. Dragging her windsor behind her, she ducked under one of the swirling masses of overhanging leaves for cover. She adjusted the black protective helmet over her head. It projected a full-sized screen onto her retina behind the visor. The night-vision setting cast a spectral green glow on her surroundings. Arleda and Thiago's silhouettes also appeared on the screen. Their bodies were reduced to blobs of neon green and orange, allowing them to stand out from the thermal imagery.

"Got it!" Arleda declared, waving the tracking device over her head triumphantly.

Eden slung the windsor over her shoulder. She joined Thiago and Arleda around a brown, dead patch of vegetation. It was a sharp contrast to its surroundings: the slight incline of a green hill covered with moss. Thiago squatted on the floor, digging out a frayed end of a piece of rope sticking out of the ground. A droplet of sweat made its way down the center of his face as he gave it a hard pull. A hidden door swung open, and he toppled back onto the ground, knocked over by his strength.

Arleda picked up the dislodged door and lay it flat on the opposite side of a gaping 4-foot-wide hole. She tapped on the side of her helmet, which matched the stripes and color scheme of her spaceship. A bright shaft of light radiated from the headlight centered above her visor, illuminating the dark opening.

"It looks like a long way to the bottom. I think it's a thirty foot drop, at least. We're looking at the location of someone who wants to say hidden," remarked Arleda. "There's only one way to find out what lies beneath. I'll jump in and send a signal if it's safe to come after me." She gave them a quick thumbs-up, nodding determinedly.

"Don't be reckless, Arleda."

Eden tiptoed over to look down into the pit. "Oh my God!" she screeched, nearly losing her balance in her shock.

As Thiago reached out to steady Eden, Arleda hopped into the opening, yelling whoops of exhilaration that echoed down the shaft behind her. After pacing around for a few painful seconds, a square band around his wrist blinked twice. He pulled up his visor and whistled.

Hercules came scampering at his master's call. The bristles of hair that carpeted his body matted together from the rain. He shook himself dry to get ready for action. Eden wasn't ready for the beast's attempt to dry himself off, and she experienced the brunt of the inadvertent attack; water splashed all over her body.

Thiago patted the creature twice on the leg. Eden watched the jumbo-sized Hercules shrink back his legs like a closing accordion, adjusting his build so he could squeeze down the hole. Thiago turned to Eden. The heels of her feet scuffed against the mud as he guided her towards the edge. Her palms were sweating as she peered down the stark black hole beneath her feet, wondering what was waiting for her at the bottom.

"Whatever you do, keep your hands at your sides at all times," Thiago instructed as he took the windsor from Eden. "Are you ready?"

"No, not really," Eden squeaked. She closed her eyes and exhaled deeply, counting to ten. It was too late to turn back now. There was nowhere else for her to go. "Okay, I'm good. I'm as ready as I'm going to be."

She clamped her arms tightly against her sides. Keeping her eyes squeezed shut, she jumped. The jittery sensation in her stomach moved up her body, to her throat and head. Her back crashed against something solid, and she started sliding. She tried to take control of her descent, but there was nothing for her to grab. As she hurtled down the chute, her body smoothly skated down spiraling twists and turns. Her breath caught in her throat. She heard someone screaming, and she realized it was herself.

"Eden! Are you okay?"

She had stopped moving. A hysterical Eden quieted down immediately, trembling as she pushed up her visor. Arleda held out a hand, her pink brows knitted together with concern. Still shaking like a diabetic low on blood sugar, Eden looked around at the dark environment of the underground cavern. Hercules tilted his head, staring at her blankly.

"Herc, you're drooling all over me," Eden groaned. She reached up to accept Arleda's extended hand. "I'm okay, thanks. Who's that behind you?"

An airborne Runic with a crossbow slung over his shoulder appeared. It was swinging a baton with a tip ablaze with flames. Although she was disoriented, the sight of an enemy was enough to shoot adrenaline into Eden's system. Even though she didn't have any feeling in her legs, she dragged herself off the floor, tackling Arleda and shoving her off to the side.

Arleda helped Eden off the ground and brushed the dust from their bodies. Without looking back, she removed a snow-white weapon with a barrel tube from her satchel. Catching sight of the barrel of Arleda's weapon, the Runic sprang off the ground with his powerful hind legs. His webbed feet stuck onto the rocky walls of the cavern with suction cups, bits of gravel crumbling under his weight. Hercules clawed at the ceiling walls with his legs, snarling ferociously at an unseen assailant overhead.

Arleda trailed the Runic with the muzzle of her blaster as he leaped from wall to wall in an attempt to avoid her line of fire. She pulled the trigger on her weapon and a bolt of bluish-white light spurted out at her target. The Runic didn't have a chance. Arleda shot him in the center of his body. His entire body changed to a block of ice within seconds. Eden watched in horror as the ice sculpture fell from the cavern ceiling like a falling icicle and splintered into bloody fragments on the floor.

Something else tumbled out of the chute. It was Eden's windsor. She seized her weapon and hauled it out of the way, clearing an area for Thiago, who landed on the ground with a thud. Before they could orient themselves, a band of Runic underlings began swarming out from the south, charging towards them.

141

"Arleda, protect Eden. I'm going to find Salabar before the bastard tries to escape."

Hercules spread his opposable limbs, swooping in on the four unfortunate Runics leading the mob. There was a sickening crunch of bone as Hercules trampled and twisted their necks. Thiago clubbed a couple of aliens out of the way, darting into the hall and out of Eden's view. As Arleda blasted ice bolts at the Runics to their left, three minions wounded by Thiago started dragging themselves towards Eden.

Eden couldn't feel her legs any longer, but she managed to hoist her windsor over her head and start to swing. Her vision filled with blinding flashes of red. Her attacks knocked the three Runics back and forth. The windsor head pierced and gouged at the alien's sides, their shrieks of anguish resounding through the cavern as they held their maimed faces.

"Eden! You can stop now!"

Eden gasped as her haze lifted. Her eyes blinked in disbelief at the bodies littered on the ground. Arleda pulled up the visor of her helmet, displaying her hand and beckoning Eden to her side.

"It's time to go."

Eden nodded wordlessly. She lifted her windsor off the ground and raced after Arleda. The pair entered a series of winding tunnels, accelerating their pace as the sounds of a struggle grew louder.

Finally, they stumbled out of the closed tube. Eden needed to hold her thighs to keep herself standing upright. She took a deep breath to soothe her wheezing. Eden's frazzled eyes darted around wildly as she tried to locate Thiago.

"Watch your step. You don't want to fall over a cliff again," warned Arleda, holding an arm out in front of Eden.

"Whoa," Eden breathed. The core of the cavern in front of them consisted of rock formations forming natural bridges and footpaths, all suspended above a hissing pit of brilliant golden-red lava.

"Up there!"

Eden jabbed a finger towards Salabar and Thiago. The tussling pair was struggling on an unbarred footpath above them. Hercules snapped his pincers helplessly; he couldn't attack Salabar without hurting Thiago. He shifted uneasily across a path that was much too narrow for his size. He struggled to keep his balance, but he was devoted to his master and refused to leave.

Thiago grunted as Salabar wriggled free from his grasp. He spotted Arleda and Eden on the ground below them. He motioned towards his weapon, which lay just a few feet away from them. He scrambled after Salabar.

"Can one of you try to stun him?"

Eden dove into the corner, grabbing hold of Thiago's weapon. She tossed it to Arleda, who snatched it in

143

midair with her gloved hands. Salabar had heard Thiago's instructions, of course. He narrowed his eyes as a look of surprise spread across his hideous features. He clenched his knotted fingers in their direction.

"You..."

Eden would never know what Salabar intended to say. Arleda fired, striking Salabar directly in the chest. Thiago's weapon was meant to kill, not stun or turn a victim to ice. A pool of red began to blossom on the thin fabric of Salabar's clothes. Small trickles of blood appeared on the corners of his mouth as he started to stagger backward.

Time slowed down for Eden as she screamed and reached out in a futile attempt to save the alien. Salabar's arms flailed as he toppled into the pit of lava.

Salabar was determined to take someone with him. His arms grabbed onto Thiago and Hercules in one final act of vengeance before his death, dragging them down with him into the fire below.

CHAPTER 18

"Thiago! Hercules!"

The imminent danger woke Eden from her slumber and forced her to take action. The apparent time shift that had cemented her in place as she watched Thiago, Hercules, and Salabar tumble over the edge shattered as quickly as it came. All that remained now was an empty platform above them with a severely chipped edge. The sweltering sea of hot lava underneath swallowed every falling piece of debris.

Eden yanked off her helmet and flung it aside. The rooms of the underground cavern reverberated with her traumatized screams of despair. She grabbed clumps of her hair, wrenching and twisting as tears seeped out the corners of her bulged, panicking eyes. Her teeth were chattering in shock as she turned to Arleda.

"How did that happen? Are they dead?"

"I don't know." Arleda wasn't moving.

Eden stared at Arleda. She hadn't known the alien for a long time, but in her experience, Arleda kept her composure and never lost her head. Perhaps this was Arleda's way of panicking. The Arkadian woman's translucent skin had turned a pasty white. The expression on her face was equally hopeless. Eden's heart sank.

"We can't stand here! Isn't there anything we can do?"

"Eden!"

Their horrified eyes moved toward the edge of their path. A cry for help rang faintly from underneath them, coupled with the unmistakable whimpers of a distressed alien arachnid. Racing to the side, they peered over the edge.

In the thick, yellow billows of smoke rising from the simmering red lava pit, Eden spotted the hazy silhouettes of Thiago and Hercules. The creature and his master were huddled together on a narrow crag protruding from a rock formation. Their arms clung to invisible handholds around them to stabilize their footing.

Eden didn't see Salabar anywhere.

"Thiago, hold on!"

Eden looked around for anything she could use to haul them up. Arleda had already sprung into action. She was stripping off thick, sturdy vines that grew wild on the cavern walls. Eden dashed off to help, positioning herself in front of another wall. She rested a boot against the rocks and wrapped her fingers around a vine as wide as a fire hose.

Her veins extruded from her neck and temples as she pulled with all her strength. She had to lean back and use both legs for leverage to make the vine finally give under her weight.

Eden carried over her small vine and handed it over to Arleda. The Arkadian bounty hunter had accumulated dozens of vines in the time it took Eden to obtain a single one, and had already knotted them all together, fashioning a makeshift rope. Thrusting one end of the rope in Eden's hands, Arleda tossed the opposite end over the cliff.

"Get ready to pull! I don't know how much longer we can safely stay on this ledge!"

Arleda positioned herself behind Eden, twisting the vines around her arms. Eden mentally ordered her uncontrollable, trembling fingers to clench, securing them around the vine. The minute, sticky fibers felt almost like velcro against Eden's sweaty palms, adhering to her flesh. Her eyes squeezed shut as the throbbing muscles in her arms started to burn from the exertion. She could feel the heels of her boots scraping against the ground. Whatever happened, she knew she could not let go.

Thanks to the alien strength built into Arleda's Arkadian genes, the women began to inch slowly backward. Incredibly, they picked up momentum, wheezing and panting as Eden passed back additional knots of the retracting vine. With one last jerk, the other end of the vine emerged. Thiago had tied it around Hercules' torso as he clutched the creature's tubby frame. Hercules grabbed at the edge, gravel crumbling under his slipping legs as he struggled to clamber onto the platform.

Thiago leaped onto solid ground. His hands never left his beloved companion's side. Arleda and Eden moved forward, each grabbing hold of one of the creature's eight limbs. Snapping his pincers gratefully, Hercules dragged himself to safety.

Everyone collapsed from exhaustion and fell flat on their backs. The group was spread out on the ground. Their outstretched arms lay limp at their sides as they recuperated. An equally exhausted Hercules slumped over on top of Thiago, bleating weakly in resignation.

Eden was the first to move. "We should get out of here," she said, squeezing Thiago on the arm as she sat up. She attempted to dust off the dirt marks on her jumpsuit, but she was a mess and couldn't clean herself. "This place is still dangerous."

"What were you thinking?"

The women jumped back in surprise as Thiago turned to confront Arleda. Unconsciously, he had made his teeth visible, and his rage was on display.

"I'm sorry. I meant to stun him. I made a mistake."

"You used to be meticulous and careful to a fault in the field. Has something changed?" he said suspiciously.

"What are you suggesting?" demanded Arleda. Anger had replaced the typical confidence in her voice. "Are you delusional enough to believe I intentionally killed him? What would I have to gain?"

Eden and Hercules exchanged worried looks as the tension escalated further.

"Guys. Let's be grateful Thiago and Herc are still alive."

"Now that the target's dead, we are only entitled to a third of the bounty," Thiago seethed, making a face as he loosened the kink in his neck. He reached into his jumpsuit and pulled out a blood-red amulet with an antique silver chain, swinging the necklace in Arleda's face. "If I hadn't taken this from the slimy bastard, we might have nothing left after expenses."

"What's gotten into you?" Arleda folded her arms over her chest and slanted her head to the right. She wasn't going to back down. "If it's the money you're worried about, you can keep my portion. I'll even transfer the difference to your account if you insist on being such a child about it."

"Thinking about the consequences of my actions doesn't make me a child," Thiago muttered. The marking on his forehead started to glow red. He nodded to himself, his head drooping forward as he emitted a low, caustic chuckle. "You haven't changed at all. In case you haven't noticed, I'm not the one who can't bring herself to call a towing service to get her absurdly overpriced spaceship repaired. I'm not the one inviting herself on an engagement when she's obviously unwanted."

"Thiago, that's enough," Eden interrupted gently. Sighing, she reached out to the alien bounty hunter. At this point, she had gotten used to and secretly fond of his affinity for frank conversation and business sense. This time, he was taking things too far. "You're starting to sound vindictive and paranoid. Come on, Thiago, everyone makes mistakes. No one's perfect. You know that."

"I'm not asking for perfection, but if you're going to tag along on my missions, you should be prepared to follow my orders," Thiago barked, running an aggravated hand through his patch of platinum-blonde hair. He kicked at the ground as he muttered angrily under his breath. A lump of rock skipped away from his boot before bouncing off the edge. "None of this would have happened if I had listened to my gut and caught Salabar on my own."

"Thiago, I understand that you're upset," said Arleda cautiously, lowering her eyes in what she hoped was a remorse stance. "You know how difficult it is for me to admit my mistakes, but you're right. I screwed it up. I'm sorry. Is that what you want to hear? If you'll let me make it up to you, I'm prepared to do whatever it takes to make it right. You have my word."

"Thanks, but no thanks," said Thiago gruffly, turning away from the women. He clicked his tongue loudly against the roof of his mouth. Hercules perked up at his master's call, his tongue wagging expectantly between his pincers. "I think we both know you've done more than your share. You can keep your damn money. I'm not interested. "

"Wait, Thiago. Where are you going?"

"I'm taking the ship to get her shields checked out. Then I'm calling a towing service to retrieve Arleda's spaceship from the service station," said Thiago as he trudged away from them. Hercules followed closely behind him.

"I think you need to get yourself examined at a hospital."

"I don't need to do anything," said Thiago, pausing by the exit. He fiddled with the square band on his wrist. "A private ship will come by to pick up you both up and bring you to the city. You probably won't want to keep the driver waiting. The meter starts running immediately."

"But Thiago..."

"No buts. All I've done is agree to compromise. We're going to start doing things my way. I'll see you in a few hours."

CHAPTER 19

"I'm stuffed," announced Eden, pulling her jumpsuit's hood over the prosthetic points of her elfin ears. She rubbed her bulging belly with both hands. "I need to walk this off."

"Seconded. I haven't eaten this much in years," said Arleda, sighing as she thought about her past. "I was the honeyberry pie eating champion at one point in my life. I consumed twenty-eight pies in three minutes. As far as I know, the record is still standing."

"Remarkable," laughed Eden, bringing her hands together in slow applause. "Someone should have erected a statue in your name for that amazing accomplishment."

"Why, thank you! I think so too," said Arleda, grinning. She slapped at her taut stomach, a hint of her sculpted abs visible through her skintight crimson jumpsuit. "Alas, those days are long gone. I usually wouldn't allow myself to ever set foot in a fast food joint like this one, but with the nightmare of a day we just had, I think it's was more than justified. "

"I hear that," Eden agreed, sniffing at the fragrant lavender aroma coming from a stall in the background. "There's just something soothing about greasy food after a long miserable day. Forget chicken soup. Fried food for the soul is where it's at."

"I can't believe I froze up," said Arleda. She exhaled bitterly, idly rubbing her shoe into the ground. "That hasn't happened to me since my first engagement."

"Don't beat yourself up about it. Things happen, even to the best of us. I know I would have fumbled if the gun were in my hands," said Eden, frowning. She paused, adding brightly, "That's why I gave it to you. For what it's worth, you're an excellent shot."

"I hope Thiago gets around to forgiving me soon."

"I'm sure he will," Eden reassured her. Eden sounded more certain than she felt. "Thiago's got a habit of storming off to take his 'walks' or run an errand whenever things get overwhelming. In all fairness, it's a pretty healthy vice if you ask me. He takes some time to calm down. He'll probably be back to his old stoic self when we see him. "

"I don't know," said Arleda doubtfully, raising a pink eyebrow. "I've never seen him that outraged before. Hold on, would you mind if we stopped in this store?"

"Not at all."

Eden strained her calves as she stood on the tips of her toes, looking with admiration at the boundless open-air flower market to her left. A giant rock arch that sparkled like purple fluorite healing crystals marked the entrance. Sitting on top of the opening were gorgeous garlands of flowers. The exotic pastels and neons were a breathtaking symphony of colors. Beyond the entryway were numerous stalls featuring a range of lush vegetation, plants, shrubbery, and miniature trees that had new sights for even the most uninhibited imagination.

"The Runic Floral Bazaar carries over eight hundred thousand species of flowers and plants imported from every corner of the galaxy," said Arleda, leading the way. "I always like to come here after exceptionally harrowing missions. It's nice to take a little break from everything I see on the job."

"I can't imagine what it's like for you."

As they ambled through the mid-afternoon crowds of the market, Eden noticed dozens of eyes looking in Arleda's direction. As both young, rubbernecking Runic men and the straying gazes of married strangers elbowed her out of the way to ogle at Arleda, Eden's face started to turn sour. She was beginning to feel like a hideously deformed monster out on a pity date with the town beauty queen. Arleda was well aware of her charm and subtle magnetic attraction for the opposite sex as she traipsed around the maze of stalls.

The 6-foot Arkadian woman was a glamorous, powerful sight. She had the buttery flow of taffy-pink hair, the blessing of infatuating curves and an ample chest she flaunted at every opportunity. Even though Eden was tall for a human woman, she never felt like she had taken command of her gangling, inherently bumbling physique. Going an entire day without walking into obstacles or tripping over her extra-long legs was a feat on its own.

Arleda led Eden to a flower cart run by an elderly Runic woman with a crooked back. The friendly woman beamed at them toothlessly as she held a pocket-sized remote in her hands. She maneuvered a large joystick with her gnarled, misshapen fingers, steering a hovering watering can with a tipped spout over her selection of bouquets and potted plants. A line of plants in the front row with bizarre flowers shaped like upturned teeth began bobbing up and down in turn under the drizzling water. The petals of the flowers looked like splatters of paint, covered in random yet cohesive colors.

All at once, the flowers split open. Wide tongues flopped about sluggishly as they lapped up water. Eden clapped a hand to her mouth in amazement.

"Arleda, my child, is that you?"

"Hello, Madame Ushera." Arleda stooped over and kissed the florist once on each cheek. She squeezed the elderly lady's shoulders, taking the remote from her. "You look younger and younger every day. I'm happy to see you using the automatic watering can I had custom-made for you."

"It has helped me immensely. Thank you again, sweetheart," said Madame Ushera, settling into a stool Arleda pulled out. "I desperately needed help watering all the plants. I couldn't have done it for much longer considering the state of my fingers. Pushing two hundred fifty years is no walk in the park, but I'm afraid you can't help how your body is when you're approaching the end of your days."

"Nonsense," said Arleda, inhaling sharply. "You're going to be around for a long time."

"Of course! Each time you visit, you add another five years to my life," the florist exclaimed. The crinkles around the florist's milky-white eyes deepened. She turned to Eden, dipping her head to get a better look under the anxious Earth woman's hood. "And Arleda, who might your friend be?"

"My name is Eden," she replied, retracting her distinctively human hands. Instead of clasping hands, Eden chose an odd, bow-legged curtsy. "It's a pleasure to meet you, Madame Ushera."

"Eden is a distant cousin from a foreign land," Arleda chipped in, swapping knowing looks with Eden.

"How nice! What a lovely relief. For a moment there, I thought your friend was one of those filthy human harlots." The Runic woman's gentle demeanor quickly disappeared.

"I'm sorry, what's that now?" said Eden, doing a double-take. She slipped a hand into her hood to ensure her elfin ears were still properly glued on.

"You heard me. You're not a part of those new-agers trying to award these whores constitutional rights, are you? I had to cut ties with my grandson when he decided to run off with a mail-order bride. Can you imagine that no-good scum trying to muck up our pure bloodlines?"

Eden had to keep her jaw forced shut. She stared at the sweet woman fondly petting the petals of the potted flowers, and couldn't believe she was capable of blatant racism. Sucking in her lips as Madame Ushera continued to murmur hateful nothings to herself, Eden found herself offended and wildly entertained simultaneously.

"Well then," said Arleda, sensing it was time to wrap up the visit. She pointed to a row of potted flowers in the back. The individual petals glittered a brilliant metallic gold as they swayed gracefully from side to side. She handed Madame Ushera a silver card. "Sadly, Madame Ushera, Eden and I are in a bit of a hurry, so we are going to have to cut our visit short. I'll take five pots of those magnificent gardzaleas. Have them delivered to my spaceship. While you're at it, make sure to charge an extra two hundred credits for yourself as well."

"Thank you, sweetheart," the florist replied, performing some operations on her computer. She handed the card back to Arleda. "Take care of yourself."

"I will, Madame. I'll see you soon."

"Sorry about that," Arleda whispered, whisking Eden off in the opposite direction. "Madame's gone a bit senile, but she means well."

"I'm sure she does," said Eden, raising her eyebrows. Hearing the sound of an adorable, toddler-like sneeze, she stopped. "What was that noise?"

She heard the delightful sneeze again and turned into the stall on her right. It came from the top left corner of an unusual selection of plants. A cluster of grape-colored orchids speckled with indigo spots immediately caught her roaming eyes. The petals shrunk back as they sniffled, the honey-yellow stigmas in the center wriggling like the wet nose of a sick puppy.

Arleda rolled her eyes. "The name's a little cheesy, but we call them cosmic orchids. Funny little things, aren't they?"

"Janine would love these," said Eden wistfully. She stroked the orchids with the back of her hand. Drawing in a sharp breath, she pinched her lips. "These are some of her favorite colors, too. It was usually the two of us and our dad together. One summer when I was fourteen, we stayed up all night painting Janine's room. Purple walls were for her study area and blue walls for the side of her bed."

"You sound like a great sister," said Arleda softly. She turned to a male Runic florist with a peppered handlebar mustache. "How much for all the orchids?"

Eden's eyes widened, placing a hand on Arleda's arm. "Oh no, please, you don't have to. It's excessive. You've paid for lunch again today, too. I really couldn't imagine more generosity."

"Don't be ridiculous," Arleda brushed her off. "I would love to get you these flowers, and I'm not taking no for an answer."

"For you, beautiful lady, only four hundred credits."

"Great. We'll take all of them," said Arleda, her silver card making its reappearance. She glanced at Eden. "Should I have all the orchids delivered to Thiago's spacecraft?"

"Sure. Wait, on second thought, would you mind if I took half of them now? I think I'd like to take them to a special place."

"Of course."

A wicker basket of cosmic orchids swung back and forth in Eden's hands as the pair wandered away from the stall. They blended into the crowd, falling behind the leisurely pace of the other market patrons. Eden dabbed at the sweat forming on the nape of her cloaked neck. It was becoming wet in the midday heat.

"Thanks again for the flowers. Thiago's ship needs some color, and these should do the trick."

"It's my pleasure." Arleda hesitated for a moment. "You know, Eden, I envy you."

"You envy me?" Eden repeated quizzically. "In which universe would you want to be in my shoes?"

"You'd be surprised. There are a few reasons. If I had to pick one, it's that you're incredibly trusting. I wish I could bring myself to have such a cheery outlook in life. It's easier said than done."

"What do you mean by trusting?"

"Oh, yes. Forgive me for being blunt, but I could never imagine myself forgiving or getting close to someone responsible for keeping me away from my family forever."

Arleda glanced sideways at Eden, who had been happy but now had a visibly downcast expression. She promptly added, "That isn't to say you shouldn't trust Thiago, of course. Forgive me if I came off that way. Apart from being one of the most skilled bounty hunters on the planet, he's one of the finest men I know. A good person, although slightly bullheaded. It's a pity we'll have to part ways sooner than I'd hoped."

"It's a shame," agreed Eden quickly, eager to change the subject. "Where are you headed next?"

Arleda narrowed her eyes, gazing at Eden intensely. "I haven't told Thiago yet. I'm not sure what he'd think of the news, but I'd love to tell you. We're friends, aren't we?"

"I don't think we're enemies."

"I was offered an amazing job out at Territory 28 in a government research base. It's a desk job. There won't be much excitement, but it pays beautifully. It took me a while to mull it over, but after some consideration, I've decided to take it. When I stumbled upon you and Thiago, I knew fate had to be working in my life. I hoped that tagging along on one of Thiago's missions would be my last hurrah before I retired completely from bounty hunting."

"That job opportunity sounds like a sweet deal," said Eden anxiously, fidgeting with her fingers. She knew Arleda was about to say something that she wouldn't like. "I'm sure you'll kick ass at whatever you do."

"I have no doubts about that. It's a shame Thiago's upset with me. I'd hate to leave just as we're becoming friends again."

Eden bit her tongue to stop herself from making any incriminating noises.

Arleda continued talking, the tone of her voice turning somber. "I've been on the road by myself for a long time. It was a pleasant surprise to have company."

Eden knew it was coming, but she could still feel sympathy stirring in her gut at Arleda's raw vulnerability. In spite of her family's numerous financial shortcomings, Eden was fortunate to grow up in a tight-knit environment with mutual love and respect, which was emotionally richer than many other people's lives. Before she could stop herself, the words came out of her mouth.

"I'll see if I can talk Thiago into coming around."

"You will? Eden, I can't thank you enough! You'll see. We'll be making unforgettable memories in no time."

"Oh, we'll be making memories all right," said Eden, feigning a smile. She gulped. The bright grin on her face vanished as Arleda turned to look away.

CHAPTER 20

The front door of Thiago's spaceship sealed shut behind him. Hercules trotted towards him at his arrival, showering his master with slobbery kisses of love and affection. Thiago reached into the pocket of his vest, sprinkling a handful of pomado prunes onto the floor. Hercules purred approvingly, diving headfirst to scarf down the treat.

As Thiago shrugged off his vest and draped it over a hanging hook by the door, the sound of feminine laughter echoed through the interior. He scowled, marching to the source of the disturbance. It was coming from the kitchen.

Arleda and Eden were both sitting on stools pulled up to the kitchen counter. They leaned their elbows against the edge as they stared at Arleda's computer propped up on the chrome finish countertop. Even as Thiago's shadow loomed behind them, they remained oblivious to their surroundings. Their eyes were pink and glazed from hours of watching the screen, intently fixed on a random intergalactic show.

"Are we enjoying ourselves?"

The women jumped up in their seats and whipped around to face him. Arleda flashed him a smile; Thiago didn't return it. She took it as a cue to leave, scooping her belongings into her satchel wordlessly and moving for the door.

"Thank you for spending the day with me, Eden. I had a lovely time. I'll see you both in the morning."

"Good night, Arleda," squeaked Eden.

Arleda sidled past an irritable Hercules and out the doorway. The door silently closed behind her. Thiago stood rigidly in place, the muscles of his jaw defined as they locked in, barely containing his wrath. His broad shoulders were eerily still, reminding Eden of the calm before an imminent storm.

"Are you going to tell me why Arleda's still here, or are we going to sit here all night?"

"Technically, you're standing," Eden began lightly. She clammed up at his withering stare. His bottom lip twitched at her weak attempt at comedy. With a sigh, her eyes fixed on the light abrasions along the toes of her boots. "I told Arleda I would try to talk you into letting her join you for your next engagement."

"When she asked if she could personally feed you a ladle of her piss, did you jump on that, too?"

"Don't be a fool. It's just one more mission before she leaves for her new desk job. Be reasonable, Thiago. She was only trying to help. She even offered to train me while you were gone. All she wants to is a chance to redeem herself."

"What is wrong with you? Are humans programmed with a genetic predisposition to always say yes? Say it with me:

N-O. No! It's not difficult. It's a part of your other favorite phrase, 'I don't know'!"

"You're being a patronizing jerk," Eden snapped. Her fists clenched together at her sides as he turned his back to her. Miffed, she leaped off the counter stool and followed him up the flight of loft steps to the bedroom. "Where are you going now?"

"Away from you," Thiago grumbled as he plopped down on the edge of the bed. He kicked off his shoes and fell back on the springy mattress, kneading his pulsing temples. Feeling the bed sink next to him underneath Eden's weight, he groaned.

"Look, I don't appreciate your habit of walking out of our conversations. Use your words."

Thiago's eyes snapped open, glaring up at Eden. "I don't appreciate you making decisions for me. Did it ever occur to you at any point to ask me first?"

"Well, okay. You have a point," said Eden, her shoulders sagging in defeat. As she leaned over, she muffled her whines of frustration as she buried her face in her hands. "You're right. I'm sorry, I don't know why I have a problem saying no to people. This is going to sound cheesy as hell, but it's in my blood. Ever since I could legally hold a full-time job, I was juggling two of them simultaneously so I could help with the bills at home. Whenever Dad needed a refill on his medication, or when Janine ran low on school supplies, I took care of it. A constant need to help people has become ingrained in my system. Now that I'm with you, I find that I'm unnecessary."

Thiago expression softened as his eyes fluttered open. His hand floated hesitantly over her lap. He began rubbing up and down her legs with enough friction to start a fire.

"Ow!" said Eden, pulling her chafing legs away from him. "What do you think you're doing?"

"I'm comforting you. Is it working?"

Eden burst out laughing. She swung out her leg and mounted Thiago, daintily draping herself over his body. Thiago wet his lips, sensing a gentle tug on his cock as the orbs of Eden's breasts swelled up against him.

Eden dragged the zipper of her jumpsuit down to her navel. Seizing his cold hands, she cupped them over her bare breasts to warm them. Her head moved around her neck sensually at Thiago's groping and gentle pinching of her sensitive nipples. It was curious how quickly Thiago had learned to pleasure Eden. He was a seasoned captain of the seas who knew just where to navigate, needing no map to locate treasure spots he'd learned by heart.

Thiago sat up, silencing her completely with a smoldering look. He lifted the tangled curtains of her hair to nibble at her neck. Eden's palpitating breaths grew louder as her nails dug into his muscular shoulders. When their hot lips found each other, they began to undress. Jumpsuits and undergarments flew across the room as the pair sloppily tumbled back into bed, sliding under the crumpled covers.

That night, Eden took control. Straddling him with her legs pinned tightly around his, she eased his cock between her dripping folds. She let loose, her butt slapping noisily against his thighs as she rode him with the stress-releasing passion of a jilted lover seeking revenge on a cheating ex. Their carnal grunts of passion were drowned out by the rhythmic banging against the steel headboard. With Thiago's attentive finger swirling against the quivering button of her clit, the pair grew closer and closer to ecstasy.

After a knee-buckling climax, Eden broke free from Thiago and collapsed into bed next to him. Clutching a hand to her sweat-covered chest, Eden rose to her feet. She gave him a sly wink, putting an extra sway to her hips as she placed a hand on one side of the bathroom doorway.

"I'm going to get myself cleaned up, and I'll be right back. You might want to warm up for round two. "

Thiago grinned, his eyes lingering on the impeccable porcelain-white flesh of Eden's naked body as she disappeared into the bathroom. As the hissing sound of the shower head drifted through the slim crack of the sliding door, he fluffed the pillow behind him and relaxed on his arms. Crossing one outstretched leg over the other, he tensed up at the sound of a sneeze.

His eyes darted to his left. A vase of cosmic orchids sat perched on his nightstand. He reached over with one finger, tickling the bright petals thoughtfully. Seeing the simple, meaningful touch of home added to the cold, unchanging interior of the spaceship he'd owned for years, the corners of his mouth began moving up.

CHAPTER 21

An alluring smell of grilled meat and broth filled the air of Thiago's spaceship. All the windows were open to air out the grill smoke, adding a pleasant tang of charred meat to the atmosphere. The table was elegantly dressed with a sheer tangerine tablecloth, brimming with buffet-style portions of toasted millie bread, juicy prong-horned boar patties, vegetables, gravy, and a large bowl of sproutpea chowder. Arleda and Eden wore aprons and full cooking gear, cleaning up the mess they made in the kitchen.

For once, Hercules neglected to ambush his master upon his arrival. Thiago glanced to his right. The creature was occupied in the living room with a pile of boar bones, slurping up and picking the succulent meat off the marrow.

Thiago tugged at his earlobe as different thoughts raced through his head. He was still upset about Salabar's death, but he knew cooking was the closest Arleda would come to asking for a truce. He'd always loved her prong-horned boar burgers, and she knew it. It was the same meal she had prepared dozens of times before. He absent-mindedly twisted a band around his wrist and cleared his throat.

"You're back," said Eden, looking up at him as she continued to polish the counters furiously.

"Come on and eat," said Arleda, beckoning at him with her freshly painted spider-black fingers. The square tips were each adorned with a single dazzling diamond. "There's plenty of food to go around."

"I see that. It all smells delicious," Thiago admitted, circling the table. He rummaged through the pockets of his satchel and removed a folded piece of rectangular card stock. He placed it on the counter and pushed it forward to Arleda. There was no emotion in his voice. "Here's your fifty percent."

"No," said Arleda, sliding the piece of paper smoothly back across the countertop. "You keep it. I don't deserve it."

Thiago didn't protest or insist that she take the money. "As you wish," he said lightly. He shrugged and slipped the check back into his bag. He pulled up an empty stool and began passing plates around the table. "To be clear, this doesn't mean I'm cutting you any slack on the next engagement."

Arleda and Eden looked at each other gleefully from across the table.

"Of course not," said Arleda quickly. She separated the bread and began creating a sandwich for herself. "Who's our next target?"

"We'll be heading to Glop territory."

Eden snorted. Both Thiago and Arleda turned to look at her. "The name is Glop? Sounds a bit ridiculous, don't you think?"

"No, I don't," said Thiago. "The reward's the same, independent of the alien race's name."

"You're going to get Katakee, aren't you," said Arleda, nodding. "That will be a good payday. Last I heard, authorities were looking to reward up to 750,000 credits for his capture."

"That was a long time ago. The premium has increased now if you can believe it."

"Wow," said Eden, whistling. She dipped a ladle into the soup bowl and served herself some chowder. "This Katakee guy sounds like a real piece of work."

"The greedy traitor sold off classified military information to the Noxx," said Arleda with a sneer, screwing up her nose. "The worst of his charges includes the theft and distribution of security equipment and explosives. The Noxx used the missile codes and any bombs they could find to wipe out entire villages for sport."

Eden's lips turned chalky white as Arleda's words registered in her mind. Her eyes flickered across the table to Thiago. He had a look of detachment on his face, but she detected a fleeting blue glow on his forehead. He didn't say anything as he finished assembling a thick burger. He pressed a gravy-soaked bun on top of the sandwich and placed it onto Eden's plate.

"How long has Katakee been on the run?"

"It feels like forever. It must be many years by this point," Arleda replied dully, cementing Eden's suspicions.

Eden bowed her head. The next mission had to play out according to the plan. There would be no mistakes allowed. She couldn't begin to imagine what capturing Katakee would mean to Thiago. He was probably the one who sold Noxx the lethal munitions used to wipe out Thiago's entire village. The attack killed his parents and everyone he knew and nearly claimed his life in the process as well.

"I understand." Eden finally spoke up. She decided a change of topic was in order. "Arleda let me use the gym on her ship to train today, and I have to say she's not going easy on me. You'd think I was training for the Olympics."

"You have to work hard to see improvement," said Thiago, cracking his first grin of the day. "Are these Olympics training for bounty hunters back on Earth?"

Eden sighed. "Not exactly. Every four years perfect physical specimens on Earth gather together to test their skills against one another and determine who is best."

"Psh," snorted Thiago, shaking his head. "That sounds stupid."

"Sorry, Eden, I'm afraid I'm going to have to agree with Thiago on that one," Arleda agreed, tossing her glossy hair away from her face to eat her food.

Eden tilted her head forward, an inquisitive eyebrow raising at their cluelessness. "Really, guys? Their job descriptions don't seem familiar to you at all? I'm going to let you two sit on that one. When I think about it, you two would be perfect candidates for the Olympics on Earth."

Arleda and Thiago feigned awkward coughs as Eden sat back, hoping for vindication.

"Eden, I'd been meaning to ask you something. What time do you think you'd be finished training with Arleda today?"

"I'm not sure. Probably a little before dinner. Why?"

"Let me know. You should probably change into warmer clothing. You'll need it where we're going."

"Just the two of us? Where exactly are we going?" asked Eden, fighting to hide a giddy smile.

"It's nowhere special. I don't want you getting your hopes up just to be disappointed. You'll just have to wait and see."

"Eden! Are you ready yet?"

"Just one minute!" Eden called out, craning her neck towards the closed bathroom door.

She turned back to the bathroom mirror and slanted her head upward. Flowering patches of her breath fogged up her reflection as she held up an eyeliner wand borrowed from Arleda. As her luck would have it, it was the one brand Arleda owned that irritated human skin. The uneven feline flicks on either side of Eden's eyes were going to be difficult to salvage.

Still, Eden didn't have to look too hard to find a silver lining. She was positive this would be Thiago's idea of a real first date. Eden wasn't about to postpone it. Arleda didn't have any way of knowing about her skin reaction, did she? The alien woman had already apologized profusely and promised the swelling would go down in the morning.

Arleda had also done a decent job with concealer on Eden. It covered up the blotchy red marks around her eyes. Instead of looking like she'd just spent hours in a tanning booth powered by the sun, frying her pasty skin to a crisp with cancerous islands of sunburn, she looked like she was trying to cover up hours of weeping.

"Screw it. This will have to do," Eden muttered hoarsely, blinking away the tears intensifying smudges of her failed eyeliner experiment.

Her makeup horror show was precisely why she opted for a nude face when possible. Not only did she lack the makeup skill other women seemed to be born with, but the hassle was too much. Flattening the ample volume of her flaming red ringlets, she did a final once-over in the mirror and plodded out of the bathroom.

"Finally," Thiago groaned. He waited for her in the living room of the spaceship. He crossed his arms and legs as he lay reclined on the couch. Hercules was curled up on the floor next to him. The creature lifted his head, whinnying idly in agreement.

"Relax, I haven't kept you waiting that long," said Eden dismissively. She accepted the helmet Thiago handed to her and looked down at it questioningly. "Are we training before the evening begins?"

"No, but put it on."

Eden placed the helmet on her head and followed Thiago out the front door of the spaceship, bidding Hercules a doting farewell with a kiss to his face. Stepping out onto the dusty ground of the campsite, she flipped up the visor of her helmet, gawking in astonishment.

A sports bike coated with frost-white paint and platinum gold finish was parked just a few feet from the doorway. In place of the oil tank was a massive puranium fuel tank. The footrest was a platform built around both the driver and passenger's seat, with extra straps and buckles to put on one's feet. Thiago dramatically checked the air pressure on the ridged tires and climbed onto the hover bike, peering over his shoulder at Eden expectantly.

"Why are you waiting? Hop on. "

"Where'd you get this?" asked Eden breathlessly, hopping onto the leather cushion of the bike. She strapped a seatbelt over her waist as Thiago leaned over to adjust her foot straps.

"It's a rental, but we're going to need it," answered Thiago. He cracked his neck from side to side, flicking switches and revving the ignition before resting his hands on the clutch. "You're probably going to want to find something to grab tightly."

"Is this thing fast, or..."

Eden's sentence cut short as the hoverbike blasted forward. As her body jerked around from the sudden acceleration, she frantically bear-hugged Thiago from behind, clasping her hands together. She buried her face into the thick black coat he wore over his jumpsuit. As the wheels of the bike slowly peeled off the floor, her heart beat rapidly against her chest.

The bike tipped backward and shot into the air, climbing thousands of feet above the ground. At this elevation, a new problem presented itself. Eden's teeth rattled in her mouth as icy gusts of wind made her start shivering. Thiago kept one eye on a computer monitor and another on the surroundings. He swerved past other airborne vehicles and accelerated to beat the building traffic.

Eden didn't know how long she clung to Thiago, but eventually her curiosity got the better of her. She braved the harsh weather around her and peeled herself away from Thiago's back, sticking her head up to peek over his shoulders. Beyond the fading clouds zipping past them was an extraordinary range of violet mountains capped with lace-white snow. She gave Thiago an ecstatic squeeze around the waist.

Eden's stomach twisted as the bike began a choppy descent. Thiago steered the vehicle toward the mountainside. He parked directly beneath the snowline near the edge of a broad mountain shelf.

"That wasn't as exhilarating as I imagined," Eden remarked. Tiny clouds of frosty breath wafted from her lips as she spoke. Eden climbed off the bike and pushed up her visor. Feeling chilled to the bone, she hugged herself in a futile attempt to keep warm.

Thiago reached into Eden's coat and pressed a button concealed in the collar of her jumpsuit. In an instant, Eden felt better about the weather. A draft of toasty warm air began to seep through the lining of her clothes. Eden exhaled blissfully. She stretched out her arms and legs, allowing the warmth to penetrate every inch of her body.

"Do all my jumpsuits have this feature? Why am I only learning about this feature now?"

"Yes, and I have no idea."

Thiago retrieved a thick blanket from the bike's storage compartment. Unrolling the blanket, he pinned it open and lay the woolen fabric on the ground, inches from the brink of the cliff. Eden joined him on the blanket as far away from the cliff as she could get. She tucked her legs underneath her as she inched closer to him for warmth.

She gazed over the edge, her mouth opening as she looked at the panorama of rainbow lights dotting the ground-level cities and floating pods. The view of the alien landscape was wonderfully picturesque against the dark late-night canvas.

"Is this where you go to cool off? The sights here are amazing," Eden marveled. She nudged him with her elbow playfully. "This isn't where you bring all your girls to get them in the mood for love, is it? Is the view one of your 'moves'?"

"Moves?"

"What you do when you want to get a woman to sleep with you."

"I've never needed any 'moves'. Women tend to sleep with me as soon as I bring them back to my ship."

"Well, good for you," said Eden bitterly, humphing.

"I suppose it is. But you're the only one I've ever brought here, if it matters to you."

"Really?"

"Yes," said Thiago, slipping a hand into the pocket of his coat. He pulled out a small black box, placing it on her lap. "Before I forget, this is for you."

Despite the frigid cold, beads of sweat formed in the creases of her palms as she picked up the container and snapped open the lid. A pair of bright, pearl-sized earrings sat on the velvet lining. It looked like a flurry of captured starlight danced inside the small baubles.

"I know it's not as flashy as any of Arleda's jewelry, but I saw these in one of the stores when I was out the other night, and I thought of you, human."

"Are you kidding?" breathed Eden. She yanked off the backs of the earrings and pierced the posts through her earlobes. "I don't know what to say. Thank you. These are the most gorgeous things I've ever seen."

"I highly doubt that, but I'm glad you enjoy them."

"Thank you so much," said Eden, flinging her arms around him in a tight embrace. "I love them."

She pushed up his visor and kissed him softly, her cold lips thawing instantly against his. Thiago kissed her back. His arms softened at his sides when her lips slowly and sensually pulled away. Eden rested her head against his shoulder, nuzzling him as she interlaced her fingers with his.

The pair gazed peacefully into the still horizon.

CHAPTER 22

"We've got all our weapons. The doors are locked, and our shields are up," Arleda said. She bent over to slip a thin dagger into the hidden compartment of her boot. "Eden, how are you doing over there? Are you ready?"

Eden shifted her hood delicately over an elaborate cinnamon-roll braid on the back of her head. A fresh breeze blew past the open flaps of her cloak, chilling the exposed parts of her body, which was almost everything. Her cleavage, stomach, and legs were visible and slathered with golden glitter. She felt ridiculous in a metal bikini top, studded with a spiral pattern of colorful jewels and precious stones.

She self-consciously started fixing her clothing. Eden tightened the knot around a matching sarong wrapped around her hips, adjusted a dangling triangular amulet on her neck, and pulled her cloak tightly around her.

She took a deep breath and held out her arms in front of her. Eden couldn't postpone this moment any longer. Arleda removed a set of handcuffs fastened to her belt and slapped them onto Eden's wrists. A soft whizzing noise emitted from the handcuffs as the teeth automatically screwed into the key holes. Arleda had Eden tightly restrained.

"Yup. I think I'm ready to go."

"We'll be back soon," Thiago called out to the window. Hercules whimpered, pawing at the door from the opposite side. "Sit tight, buddy."

"That's sweet," said Eden. Her body awkwardly moved as Thiago led her away from the ship. He held the handle of the leash to her shackles. "Poor Hercules can't stand being away from Thiago."

"Thiago and that thing are inseparable," Arleda concurred. She flashed them a sheepish grin. "Bless his heart."

"I rarely go on a mission without Herc by my side," said Thiago, cutting through the Glop city square and moving toward a secluded alley. "He'll need to stay behind this time or we'll risk blowing our cover."

As they dragged Eden through the alleyway, she found she had to start jogging to keep up with Thiago's driven pace. She glanced around at the jarring crimson color illuminating the long, narrow stretch of the Glop red light district. Shadowy entrances to strip clubs and seedy love motels advertised with neon signs lined the lane. Although the signs were overwhelming at first, careful inspection revealed their age. Some were missing multiple LEDs, and others had electronic marquees that only scrolled halfway through the screens.

Wedged between the esteemed gentlemen clubs were tall, clear booths with glass tinted in different shades of red and pink. Eden's jaw dropped wide open as she openly ogled the unusual features of the female representatives of the Glop race. All sense and good manners flew right out the window.

The alien women were six feet tall, at least. They wore fancy brassieres, nipple pasties, and skimpy thongs. They had surprisingly human-like skin tones and looked like overgrown sumo wrestlers. Rings covered bewitchingly loose bodies, reminding Eden of the Michelin tire mascot. She watched with a combination of revulsion and fascination as the Glop women danced to thumping music blaring out their speakers. Thankfully, only a few flashed them, seductively rubbing their pumpkin-sized breasts against the glass.

"Well, we're here," Thiago whispered, stopping at an old, three-story establishment tucked away at the end of the alley. He tugged on Eden's shackles, drawing her close to him. "Whatever you do, don't say anything. If you do as they tell you, and stick to the plan, you'll be fine."

"You'll be more than fine," Arleda reassured her, squeezing her once on the elbow. "You're going to be great."

Eden looked anxious as Thiago knocked twice with the back of his knuckles on a dark wooden door. The door swung open, revealing a striking Noxx madam at the threshold. She had neatly pulled back the crown of white feathers around her head. Black rings outlined her hypnotically amber eyes. A plum, floor-length gown complete with a lace-trimmed train covered the white scales on the bottom half of her body. As the Madam's

181

intense eyes settled on Eden, she felt intimidated and dropped her inquisitive gaze to the ground.

"Madam Cecilia?"

"Who the hell are all of you?"

"My name is Arleda, and this is my associate, Thiago. We contacted you last night about the potential bride we would like to offer your esteemed establishment. We've brought her here, as per our discussion, to see if she will meet your requirements. May we come in?"

Eden squealed in surprise as Madam Cecilia's cold fingers curled around her wrist and forced her forward. She was so frightened she couldn't move. Eden's shoulders became tense as the Madam slid the cloak off her shoulders. Eden's body was not her own any longer. She was twirled around for an inspection, and she was helpless.

The Noxx leaned closer and sniffed her like she was a slab of meat. Next, the madam cupped one hand around Eden's butt and the other on a breast. The stranger squeezed freely, handling Eden's private areas like she was an animal.

Eden had to resist the urge to retaliate for the blatant sexual harassment. Madam Cecilia stepped back and lifted her nose into the air. Her wrinkled lips pressed together. She didn't say anything, but went to the front door and held it open for the group. The trio walked in single file through the doorway.

The heart of the brothel was a blunt contrast to the dismal facade, which looked similar to a drug den when one looked at it from the outside. The interior was spotless and extravagant. Classic gothic furniture filled it, which gave it a regal atmosphere. A carpeted winding staircase led to a series of soundproof rooms. Green and red lights fixed to the doors indicated if the rooms were vacant or occupied.

Paintings featuring generic nature scenes adorned the walls, complementing the romantic floral backdrop of the wallpapers. Soft jazz played from the overhanging speakers. There was even a receptionist behind a counter, complete with a silver bell and a sophisticated centerpiece on the desktop. If it weren't for the interracial mix of alien women in frilly dresses and lingerie lounging around as they waited for the next customer, the building would look like a perfectly quaint bed and breakfast.

"How much are you looking for?" Madam Cecilia inquired coldly, stroking her chin.

"How much do you think she's worth?"

"She's a little bony, but our supply of natural redheads is running low. Forty thousand? Sixty if her hymen's intact."

Eden felt conflicted. On one hand, the casual sex slave bidding war in front of her was revolting. On the other, she was offended that she wasn't even worth six figures.

"We're willing to negotiate. Why don't we have someone test her out first, free of charge," Arleda offered. She wiggled her eyebrows suggestively. "You know some of your regulars are willing to pay excessive amounts for just an hour with a freshly captured human bride. If the client is fully satisfied, you'll have to cough up eighty. If anything goes wrong, and there's the slightest complaint, we'll hand her over for twenty."

"Are you proposing a bet? I do like to play games," Madam Cecilia drawled. She grabbed hold of Eden's chin and forcibly tilted her head upward, tracing her bejeweled four-inch-long stiletto nail along the human woman's quivering flesh. "There's no sign of age lines on her neck. She's a young one." Madam Cecilia looked off into the distance. "I believe she'll fit in quite nicely here."

"What about him?" said Thiago, gesturing to a Glop checking in at the counter.

It was Katakee. The unsightly alien leaned against the countertop as he attempted to chat up the cowering receptionist. With a short, pencil-thin mustache, an oily orange comb-over, and a baby-blue suit emblazoned with half-naked alien women custom made to fit his hulking figure, the cocky fugitive was a peculiar marriage of creepy and weird.

"I believe I've won this bet already. You may be out of luck. That gentleman is one of our best customers. He's also one of the pickiest," said Madam Cecilia, cackling darkly. "Very well, I'll go ahead and make the arrangements."

The train of the Madam's dress trailed after her like a sea of purple snakes. The trio observed carefully from a distance as the Noxx woman exchanged hugs with Katakee. Madam Cecilia and Katakee said quick pleasantries before the madam leaned in close to the Glop fugitive, speaking in hushed tones.

"Are you okay, Eden? You look a little green," said Thiago softly, glancing sideways at her. "Are you sure you can do this?"

"Of course. I'm all right," insisted Eden with false conviction. She fought to keep her voice from trembling. The handcuffs suddenly seemed too tight on her wrists.

"Don't worry," said Arleda, lowering the volume of her voice as Katakee and Madam Cecilia started to head back in their direction. "We'll be right outside the door. It will be just like we practiced."

"Okay."

Katakee grabbed the handle of Eden's leash from Thiago's hands. Madam Cecilia led the way up, ushering Eden and the client towards a suite on the second floor. As Arleda and Thiago began following them up the flight of steps, Katakee grunted disapprovingly, snarling at the madam.

Madam Cecilia got the message. "The client wants you to wait for him downstairs."

"Not a chance," said Thiago immediately. "We need to stand guard by the door to ensure the goods aren't damaged. If we can't protect our investment, the deal is off. "

Katakee clucked his tongue indignantly. He ultimately relented. As they reached a room located at the far end of the hallway, the Glop swept Eden off the ground by the waist and slammed the door shut in their faces. Arleda and Thiago nodded at each other briefly, moving to the side of the twin doors as Madam Cecilia sauntered away from them.

Eden gagged as the stench of an overflowing dumpster on a hot summer's day emerged from Katakee's puckered lips. Removing the hood over her head, he wrapped his chubby, brawny arms around her waist. His cold tongue flopped lazily along the contours of her cleavage. Eden tried not to move, but she couldn't help attempting to escape. Katakee quickly grew tired of her squirming and writhing. He shoved her onto a king-sized double bed.

Eden rolled onto her side. She silently watched as Katakee turned his back to her and prepared to disrobe. He laid his concealed weapons down on the coffee table before stripping off his clothes. She clenched her lips and didn't make a sound. Eden focused and lifted her shackled hands to the amulet around her neck. When she gave a small button concealed in the back of the pendant a hard jab, an antique key ejected from a triangle in the center of the necklace. She caught the tiny key with the tips of her fingers and gently fit it into the keyhole in her handcuffs. When Katakee had removed his clothes and turned back around to face her, Eden was already free from the restraints. She bent over to retrieve a laser tucked inside her boot.

Their eyes met across the room, widening simultaneously. Katakee's eyes were frightened, but Eden's eyes were full of anticipation.

"Now," she shouted.

Thiago and Arleda burst through the doors on cue, fully armed and ready for destruction. The startled Katakee whirled around with his hands up in surrender and his boxers halfway down his knees. Eden never got the laser out of her shoe; it refused to budge. She rolled off the bed and crashed onto the floor, making sure to keep herself out of the line of fire.

Eden struck her head against the post on the foot of the bed. As her sight began to blur, she saw Katakee's shadowy figure freeze solid like an awkwardly-posed mannequin and topple forward to the floor with a loud thud.

CHAPTER 23

Back on the ship, Eden was hungry again. She squirted healthy servings of sweet butter frosting onto a tray of millie flour cupcakes. Eden scooped up some of the cream with her fingertips and passed it between her lips, licking contentedly. As she tipped back her head and opened her mouth wide to squirt frosting into her mouth straight from the can, a chiming of bells rang through Thiago's spaceship.

"Arleda's here!"

Thiago emerged from the bathroom, wiping wet hands on his sides as he headed to the door. Arleda entered the ship, balancing a basket of hot meals on top of arms filled with bulging paper bags. Thiago and Eden rushed to help her, brushing away a snooping Hercules. He attempted to poke his head into Arleda's belongings.

"Thank you. I did not want to make two trips," said Arleda, setting the rest of the bags on the kitchen counter.

"I know what you mean," Eden piped up. "I do the same thing with my groceries."

"What is all this stuff?" Thiago's brows furrowed as he browsed through the contents of the bags. The glass bottles clinked against each other noisily as he checked the labels. "There's enough liquor in here to get a small nation blitzed out of their minds. Are you throwing a party? Let's hope it is back on your ship, because I didn't authorize anything like this."

"Of course not," Arleda scoffed, rolling her eyes. "It's all for us. I think our victory calls for a grand celebration, don't you? Katakee is behind bars, where he belongs. We're all a lot richer now."

"You guys got the authorities to close down that horrible brothel, too," said Eden. An involuntary shudder gripped her body at the thought. "I couldn't believe all those poor human women locked away in the basement. They'll be sent off to a rehabilitation center for recovery before they decide what they want to do."

"It was one of our better engagements," Thiago conceded. "But your purchases are inappropriate. Did you forget humans are deathly allergic to alcohol on this planet?"

"Oh, no, that's okay. You guys go ahead and partake as much as you want. You deserve it. I'm happy to babysit."

"I'm offended you think I would ever forget about Eden," Arleda interjected smugly. Stuffing her hand into one of the bags, she rifled through to the bottom. Her fist emerged moments later, dangling a clear bag with nuggets of dark purple bud covered with fuzzy yellow hair. "Dolly grass is all-natural and a hundred percent human-friendly. I guarantee it."

Thiago selected an alternative instrumental playlist to play over the speakers. The relaxing mood music had a pacifying effect on the trio sprawled on the couch. As Arleda filled two glasses of Pasquin ale to the rim of the glass, Thiago instructed Eden on how to pack a healthy, hard-hitting dolly joint.

There was a vanilla flavor to the wrapping paper as he sealed the joint shut. He pressed the finished product to his lips and lit up the other end. Faint tufts of purple smoke were floating through his parted lips. He passed it over to Eden to begin the cycle.

Within an hour, all three were deliriously happy, reveling in different levels of buzz. Eden rose from the couch, a numbing head rush coursing through her body as she stood up. She jumped over Arleda and Thiago's stretched legs on the coffee table. Her thin frame swayed side to side in drowsy glee. The heavenly weed completely alleviated the soreness in her legs. She felt like she was walking on a patch of fluffy, airy clouds as she tread gingerly on the carpet. She practically levitated to the bathroom.

Some time later, Eden stumbled out of the toilet after a fierce struggle with her jumpsuit zipper. As she bumbled her way back to the couch, the carefree smile stretched across her face swiftly vanished. Her knees buckled against each other. Her legs suddenly felt softer than gelatin. Every instinct in her body told her to look away, but she couldn't. Instead, her eyes locked onto a heart-twisting scene.

She stared blankly at Arleda and Thiago, who had their lips locked in an intense kiss. As Thiago slowly became aware that he was being observed, he pulled away from Arleda. His eyes widened in horror at the sight of the shell-shocked Eden, standing just a few feet away.

Eden was suddenly able to move her legs again.

"Eden, wait!"

Ignoring Thiago and Arleda's pleading cries, she stomped on the pedal attached to the wall of the doorway. Before either of them could stop her, she slipped through the jaws of the opening doors and vanished out of sight.

CHAPTER 24

FIVE MINUTES EARLIER

A dense violet fog cloaked Thiago's ship. The sound of mellow beats playing in the background made him unconsciously turn his head from side to side. The sweet warmth of the Pasquin ale toasted his body from the inside out. The mild spasms of muscle pain that were always present in a bounty hunter's body had decided to take a temporary vacation. He felt like a billionaire tycoon lounging around at a secret hideaway.

The capture of Katakee was still a recent success in everyone's mind. All three of them had followed the plan to near perfection. It was one of those rare moments teamwork had worked for Thiago. He couldn't remember the last time he had allowed himself to relax this freely. There was always something else that needed to be taken care of or a project he could work on to get ahead.

Not at this moment. Right now, his only concern was pouring himself another shot of ale which he hoped would lull him to sleep.

The couch squeaked underneath Thiago as he shifted in his seat. He kept the heels of his boots hooked on the edge of the coffee table as he rested his palms flat on his stomach. As his drooping head nodded sideways, his eyelids began to close.

"Thiago."

His head snapped upright. He was dazed and blinking sleepily as his head slowly turned to his left. Arleda reclined on his couch like an Egyptian queen sitting on a chaise lounge throne. In the silence, he had nearly forgotten her presence.

Arleda delicately draped one leg over the other. Purple wisps of smoke drifted from her lips in the shape of little hearts. She offered the blunt to Thiago between her fingers. The chubby spliff was burning midway through its length. She subtly nudged her prominent cleavage closer together with her arms. The Arkadian marking on her forehead glowed a sensual red.

"No thanks," said Thiago hoarsely. His throat felt prickly and dry from all the dolly grass. Groaning, he reached over clumsily to refill his goblet.

"Hold your horses, Thi-ger. Let me get that for you before you make a mess of yourself."

Arleda intercepted his hand, giving him a quick squeeze on the knee to stop him. She tipped the remnants of an open bottle of ale into his goblet. As she handed the glass to him, her hand lingered on Thiago's leg. Her bedazzled spider-black manicure was so pristine that her nails looked unrealistic. But in Thiago's blissful stupor, he failed to notice. His head tilted back against the back of his couch as he accepted the goblet and swallowed the contents in one go.

"Thanks," he muttered. A loud burp came out of Thiago's mouth. He wriggled his legs away from her prying grasp. As he set his goblet back down on the table, a muted clang sounded from behind the closed bathroom door. He heard a quick reshuffling of objects followed by Eden's cheery voice.

"I'm okay!"

"Did you fall in the toilet again?" Thiago hollered towards the bathroom, one hand lazily cupped around the side of his mouth.

"What do you mean *again*? I can't get my zipper to close. It's complicated! I'll fix it and be out in a second!"

"Eden's fine. She's a big girl," said Arleda tartly. She swiftly softened, forcing herself to smile. "And a strong one, at that. I have to admit, Thiago, I sincerely admire you for deciding to accept her. It takes a rare man to treat his charity case with such respect and kindness."

"Charity case?" Thiago repeated. His voice grew wary. "That's not a term that has ever crossed my mind."

"What would you call her, then?" Arleda scoffed. She couldn't mask the scorn in her throaty chuckle. Arleda suddenly stopped twirling her hair. The silky strands of bubblegum-pink uncoiled from her fingers. "I assumed you were fucking her because she was available. Never in my wildest dreams would I imagine the great Thiago Arris would have feelings at all, much less for a human girl."

"I think I've missed the part where this concerns you," said Thiago firmly. There was an air of finality to his voice. "This conversation is over. Let's move on."

"Oh, Thi-ger. I haven't upset you already, have I? You know what a kidder I am. What has gotten into you?"

"I'm not upset, but I think a change of topic would be beneficial for both of us."

"Let me rephrase things," Arleda drawled. She couldn't let the subject drop as she inched closer and closer to Thiago. He tried to move back, but sidling any further away from her would make him fall off the edge of the couch. "What I meant to say was that I think you're an inspiration for what you're doing here with Eden. It's revealing a new aspect of your personality I've never seen before. You have grown so much since we last parted ways."

"Evidently you haven't," Thiago replied coldly. The hair lining his arms stood up straight as a feeling of uneasiness stewed in the pit of his stomach. "Would you mind moving over a little? There's plenty of room on your end of the couch."

"Come on, Thiago," Arleda persisted. She sighed wistfully, her warm breath teasing Thiago's burning earlobes. "All I'm saying is, taking down Katakee was a rush. Didn't it bring back any memories of us and how well we worked together?" She slid her hand around his arm.

"Arleda, you need to let go of me," Thiago warned.

Thiago was quickly sobering up. His temples were pounding like a military drillmaster was screaming in his ears. He attempted to withdraw his arm from Arleda's iron grip, but her fingers only tightened around his wrist. Her nails clawed into his flesh, and she drew him in, smashing her lips against his. The sticky coating of her gilded gloss smeared against his closed mouth.

The timing was terrible, but Thiago heard the clear-cut clicking of the bathroom door as it unlocked. Eden's horrified face appeared in front of him. Thiago's sense of urgency overpowered Arleda's pure Arkadian strength, and he shoved her off onto the floor.

"Eden." Thiago's eyes were starting to water from the mixture of both smoke and the constant throbbing in his head. He staggered to his feet despite being dragged down by the anchor of Arleda's grasp.

The commotion woke up Hercules. The creature's eight legs teetered sloppily underneath him as he scrambled uncertainly to his feet. He didn't know what was happening, but he had gone from slumber to action in a moment. Hercules yapped instinctively in Thiago's defense as he became agitated in his nest tucked away in the corner of the living room.

"Eden, wait!"

When he finally managed to escape from Arleda's pawing hands, Thiago looked up to see the spaceship's front door sealing shut. Hercules' whimpers of confusion filled the now-silent room. The loyal creature trotted towards Thiago, burrowing his head into his brooding master's side. Perhaps sensing the Arkadian woman's contribution to the drama around him, Hercules snarled unpleasantly at Arleda when she rose from the couch behind them.

Thiago stamped on the door pedal and slipped through the doorway with Hercules and Arleda following closely behind him. Veins in his neck bulged in frustration as he paced around the spaceship. He searched all around the ship, but there was no trace of Eden.

"Let her go, Thiago. You know how emotional humans can get. If you give her a little space and some shiny things, Eden will be back to her old self." Arleda reached out to gently take his arm.

"Get out of my sight," Thiago hissed. He pulled himself away from Arleda and vaguely pointed in a random direction.

"Wait a minute, Thi-ger," said Arleda pleadingly. Her nervous laughter faded away when she saw the look of fury brewing in Thiago's eyes. "You don't mean that, do you?"

Without speaking, Thiago reached into his boot and pulled out a concealed laser pistol. He pointed the barrel of the bronze weapon straight at Arleda. Despite his intoxicated state, his outstretched arm remained perfectly still.

"I think I do."

Arleda stared at the muzzle of Thiago's gun before raising her eyes to meet his. She opened her mouth as if she were about to say something, but decided against it. Whipping her hair over her shoulder, she lifted her nose into the air and complied. Trying to keep her composure, she marched away to her spaceship as her hips swayed and heels clicked into the night.

Muttering indescribable words filthy enough to make a sailor blush, Thiago threw his weapon onto the ground and returned to his ship.

"What do you know? I went all the way to the other side of the galaxy just to discover that men are still dogs over here."

Eden grumbled under her breath as she marched down the barren badlands of Glop territory. Avian squawks that sounded like a pack of wounded cats pierced through the darkening skies overhead. Glancing up at the vulture-sized, two-headed alien birds circling above her, Eden sped up her pace. She didn't know if they were waiting to eat her, and she didn't want to find out.

A chilly breeze blew past her. In the process of storming out of Thiago's ship in such a heated, mindless rush, she had forgotten to put on her coat and a sensible pair of shoes. She absently reached behind her collar in a futile search for the self-heating button on her jumpsuit, which she wasn't wearing.

Looking down at her outfit only further incited Eden's rage. She wore the designer ensemble Arleda had lent her for their party. The sleeveless halter jumpsuit patterned with pastel sequins looked better than it felt. Shivering, Eden wrapped her arms around herself, aimlessly heading north.

As she walked, she realized something unusual. There were no signs of life around her other than the alien birds patrolling the skies. All she saw was emptiness. There were no peaceful drifters, no Xorxes junkies...not even a single unrecognizable landmark in sight.

Eden's shoulders slunk down in dismay. Images flashed in her mind that she did not want to see. Her upper lip twitched at the thought of Arleda's hands wrapped firmly around Thiago's chin. She saw their lips locked together in the heat of uncontainable passion. She shook her head, flapping a hand in front of her face like she could physically remove the picture etched into her retinas.

The fact that the intimidating pair looked effortlessly beautiful together was an extra slap in the face. Did the aliens belong with each other? They had all the chemistry of a Grecian deity power couple.

It wasn't merely Thiago's inability to keep his hands to himself that bothered her. Eden was mad at Arleda as well. She couldn't help feeling foolish for believing, however briefly, Arleda was her friend. Arleda was the only female she could turn to for advice on this planet.

In hindsight, Arleda had not been subtle about her desires. It was always clear Arleda's lingering feelings for Thiago were more than "former work partners." But even though Eden had never verbalized her relationship with Thiago, Arleda should have respected her boundaries.

As Eden gazed at the never-ending path that stretched in front of her, a wave of rationality came crashing down. It occurred to her that she hadn't given Thiago or Arleda a chance to explain themselves.

Eden thought about the lightheadedness that came as an aftereffect from the dolly grass blunts the trio had consumed. For Eden, she struggled just to get the zipper of her jumpsuit working correctly. Additionally, Thiago and Arleda had both drained three bottles of Pasquin ale in less than two hours.

Being under the influence was no excuse for their actions. But the more Eden thought about it, the gravity of their drunken indiscretion grew less severe. She wasn't thrilled with what happened or ready to forgive, but the notion of leaving everything behind seemed silly. Her brain was racing in circles, making up answers to her questions.

More to the point, where could she run? Earth was a long walk away.

Eden felt like a runaway child with an empty piggy bank and nowhere to go. She would have to make the long trek back home. She spun around indignantly, squinting in the distance. The faint tracks of her walk marked a path back to the campsite. With a sigh, she grudgingly began to retrace her steps.

"Eden!"

Eden looked up. Her ears burned red when she heard Arleda's voice. The Arkadian woman approached from the distance, her lustrous hair swishing in the wind like a shampoo commercial. The sight of Arleda brought Eden's temper rushing back. She cast Arleda a withering look before stomping away from her.

"Is this some more of your charity? Thanks, but no thanks. You didn't need to get me. I'm a big girl. I'll find my way back to the ship by myself."

"Eden, wait. Can you just hear me out?"

"About what? I'm not interested in learning the rules of alien girl code."

She felt a sharp pain in her leg. Eden's mouth went silent as she looked down to see the sharp needle of a syringe dart sticking out of her thigh. She gasped, finding it hard to breathe as she grabbed frantically at her throat. As the last drop of lime-green liquid inside the syringe disappeared, Eden's legs started to buckle under her. She crashed into the ground. Her icy limbs solidified as paralysis gradually took over her body.

Arleda grabbed Eden's cold ankle and started dragging the immobilized human away to her spacecraft.

CHAPTER 25

A balding man wearing horn-rimmed glasses and a flannel shirt too large for his slim frame sat cross-legged upon the bank of a glittering pond. He held an old fishing pole between his legs and began to patch up the bait cast with silver masking tape. Satisfied, he looked over his shoulder, patting a vacant patch of grass next to him. A warm smile illuminated his sunken face.

"Come sit next to me, Eden."

Eden toddled over to the man using her stumpy legs. The man scooped her up just before her overexcited little legs sent her toppling over the brink of the bank. He set her down next to him, gently placing the hook of the fishing rod in her small palms. The child dug into the tub of live bait next to her. She giggled at the tiny creatures squirming against her fingers. The man took the wiggling bait from her and fixed it onto the hook.

"Are you ready, Eden?" the man asked. He placed his arms over hers, guiding her movements. "Remember what I told you. You have to flick your wrist back and then push forward."

"Okay."

"When you feel a nibble, what do you do?"

"I watch the line in the water. Then I pull."

"That's right. Go ahead. You can do it, Eden."

The tip of Eden's tongue poked out from the corner of her mouth as she concentrated. The man removed his arms from her and allowed the child to cast the rod on her own. The tip of her rod dipped into the water with a soft splash. The bright red fishing bobber bounced on the rippling surface of the pond. Within mere seconds, her arms tugged forward at an unmistakable nibble on the other end of the line. The little girl's eyes popped wide open in gleeful excitement.

As the indicator line around the bobber sunk under the water, Eden pulled with all the giddy gusto of a young child. Water splashed around her as a thrashing fish jumped out of the surface and soared through the air, landing next to her. She glanced down at the fat rainbow trout flopping on the ground. It was nearly two feet from nose to tail. Beaming with pride, she turned around to brag about her capture.

"Dad, did you see what I just did? Dad?"

There was no answer.

Eden twirled around in panic. The man was gone. Her bottom lip began to tremble. She got up and began to look for her father. No matter how hard she tried to retrace her steps, her ruffled socks and Mary Janes only seemed to move around in circles.

Giving up, the child fell onto the cushion of the grass below her. As her eyes settled on the trout next to her, she tilted her head slightly to the side.

The shadows of an Arkadian symbol could be seen on the scales of the dead fish.

The pungent stench of sulfur blew into Eden's nostrils. She slowly woke up. It was a burden to lift her head from her shoulders. But as she sluggishly came to, numbing waves of hysteria washed over her system.

She found herself trapped in a vertical cage suspended high above the ground. A sturdy pair of handcuffs restrained her hands over her head. They were designed to impede all wrist movement.

The rusty chains dangling from the ceiling gave her a small amount of movement in her legs. A separate pair of restraints held her ankles in place. Everything was designed to keep her thrashing to a minimum. The muscles in her limbs nagged at her for depriving them of rest as she fought to keep herself standing up.

Eden inspected the walls of the cage with a sinking heart. Ominous bolts of red electricity sparked between the spaces of the black bars. She had as much chance of escaping containment as a roasted duck hanging in the display window of a Chinese restaurant.

She puckered her lips as she breathed loudly through her mouth. She tried to keep her mind calm as she studied her surroundings. The walls around her cage contained rows of capsules reaching higher than she could see. She stretched her neck forward, straining to get a better look at the mysterious vessels. They had a thick, gelatinous liquid the murky color of mucus and something Eden couldn't comprehend.

When she realized what was in the capsules, she gasped in shock. Along with a handful of humanoid captives, different races of aliens occupied the containers. The capsules permanently preserved their final haunting expressions before death. Eden tore her eyes away from the gruesome graveyard. She fought back the sour taste of bile rising in her throat.

The sprouts of moss growing from damp spots on the crumbling cavern walls suggested she was underground. As she saw dozens of uniformed Noxx officials pouring in through a doorway on her right, she realized where she was.

Bounty hunters had been on a quest to uncover the lair of the Noxx army for years. She was in the middle of it. Thiago would love this place if he could ever find it.

"Hey, assholes! Let me out of here!" Eden said in disgust.

Eden pulled back as her gob of spit bounced off the sparking cage bars and deflected back on her face. The heads of the aliens shifted up to listen to the shrieks of the human prisoner. One was startled more than the others. The bungling official struck the back of his head on a hanging wall fixture. He reeled over dizzily before another alien swooped in and caught him.

"You! You there with the lazy eye! Stop acting like you can't hear me. I know you can. Go ahead, guys, walk away from me all you want. I've got a whole playlist of horrible pop songs in my arsenal, and I'm not afraid to use them! I'll give you a fair warning. I can't carry a tune to save my life."

The Noxx officials continued as if she hadn't said anything. A few shielded their ears to block out Eden's obnoxiously shrill voice. She cleared her throat theatrically. When she started belting the tune to one of her favorite childhood TV shows, a few aliens cried out boisterously in protest.

Eden's mouth shriveled shut as the door to the central entryway opened. A Noxx dressed in a unique set of black army fatigues strode into the room. He was much taller than the guards. In addition to the Noxx's imposing height, there were distinctive chocolate-brown markings shaped in a lopsided V between his eyes. Before, the officials were at ease. After their superior entered, they quietly moved to form neat lines.

Arleda quickly joined him. "I'm interested to know your thoughts on the cargo, Malatov."

The pair ascended a long flight of steps leading to the pedestal on which Eden's cage rested. Eden cowered before them, burying her face in her arms as the pair leaned in and examined her. Malatov snarled, his guttural roar frightening everyone as it echoed through the space of the underground cavern.

"Look at me."

Involuntarily, Eden's head moved up from her arm. Disobeying the commanding voice was difficult. As Malatov sized her up, she couldn't stop her teeth from chattering. At this proximity, the Noxx leader was worse than she had imagined.

Malatov probed her with his fiery amber eyes. The one on his left was sewn partially shut and only exposed a sliver of a congealed, severely infected eye socket. The grayed feathers that adorned his head drooped from age. Exquisite, time-worn tattoos covered the gleaming white scales of the bowling ball-sized muscles bulging from his arms.

Arleda beamed alongside him. She sneaked a cheeky wink in Eden's direction. The Arkadian woman's hair was pulled away from her face in a sleek ponytail, displaying her beautiful chin and close-lipped smile in its full glory.

"Are you sure you've brought me the correct tramp? This one's human, for goodness sake."

"Trust me, this is the one. It looks like Thiago's got himself a new fetish for Earth skanks. The half-breed's finally showing his true colors, I suppose."

Malatov laughed huskily in agreement. He stroked his chin. A flake of skin peeled off his pink snout as he sniffed Eden.

"She's little on the lean side. I don't like her hair, but she smells as sweet as my last kill."

"I can guarantee that Thiago will be looking for her very soon. He'll come directly to you. When he arrives, you and your men are free to finish him off."

Eden gasped. "Arleda, why are you doing this?" she asked. Her voice sounded more brittle than she had intended. "How could you? With him? Look at him!"

"Don't take it personally, sweetheart. It's just business," Arleda replied promptly. The nasty tone of her voice sent an unpleasant tingle down Eden's spine. "You're a smart girl. Keep your head up. For what it's worth, I did like you. If you need to why, it should be obvious. Malatov is offering much more than any of the pitiful rewards the authorities are willing to fork over."

"You greedy, two-faced bitch."

Arleda stuck a hand on her hip and motioned to a new, ring-pop sized jewel on the little finger of her free hand. "That may be, but I've just bought myself a nice little treat worth more than your life ever will be. It only cost a quarter of what I received for escorting you here. The ring's not too flashy, is it? What do you think?"

"I think you should take that ring and jam it up your mom's hole in case she spawns any more of Satan's babies."

"Feisty girl!" Arleda rolled her eyes. "When you have no weapons left, all you can do is use your mouth."

Malatov stuck a hand through the bars of the cage to caress the supple skin of Eden's burning cheeks.

"I can see why the bastard's got a soft spot for her. She's attractive, in a primitive sort of way."

Eden whipped her hair around her face as she pulled away from Malatov. Her shackles clanged together. Two small spiders crawled out from Malatov's sleeves, crossed the bridge of his crooked yellowing fingers, and leaped onto Eden's twisting neck.

As his fingers approached her contorting lips, Eden reacted instinctively. She clamped her jaw over two of his fingers, chomping down as hard as she could.

"Son of a bitch! Get off of me, you disgusting human!"

There was a loud crack as Malatov's knuckles connected with Eden's cheek. Her head slumped to the side of her neck. She couldn't believe the viscous display of force. Malatov withdrew his arms from the cage, angrily setting the voltage of the cage bars to its highest setting.

As a bickering Arleda and Malatov wandered down the flight of steps and away from her, Eden couldn't control her emotions any longer. Sobbing, Eden quietly cried herself to sleep.

CHAPTER 26

A woman's gentle modulated voice wafted out the speakers of the shuttle cars.

This is a safety announcement from the staff at the HT-007 Inter-territory Shuttle System. Constant video recording is in effect for the security of both our staff and our passengers. We would like to remind patrons not to leave luggage or any belongings unattended. Abandoned belongings will be confiscated by security personnel and destroyed immediately without further notice.

The air was thick with the musky sweat, body odor, and tentacle secretions of traveling passengers. In the after-work rush hour, the light chatter and pleasantries were muffled by the rhythmic whoosh of the ISS zipping through the tunnels. Most passengers were quiet. They were exhausted from a day's work. Some stared blankly into space with dead eyes; they kept their hands idly folded in their laps. Others snored loudly in their seats or slept standing up, resting their heads on their arms as they steadied themselves with hanging straps.

Thiago loitered close to a door in a back of a congested car, leaning against a ridged wall. He was unprepared when the shuttle made an abrupt turn to the left. He collided with an Azkal next to him, who was already in a foul mood because his face had smashed against the ceiling. Thiago mumbled a quick apology and evaded the alien's six glowering eyes by tugging a hood over his head.

A lifetime of social skills left unpolished had resulted in the enhancement of Thiago's naturally agoraphobic tendencies. He couldn't recall the last time he had been aboard public transportation. With the notorious stigma and unabashed racism that followed half-humans, he had grown accustomed to keeping a low profile. It was impossible to feel safe in a crowd without his cloak, or, at the very least, a prosthetic disguise to conceal his nature.

Today, he opted to leave Hercules and his spaceship parked back at the campsite in case Eden decided to return. If he'd learned anything from their past disagreements, it was that it was best to keep himself at a distance until Eden's anger subsided on its own.

After a long period of contemplation, Thiago had enough sense to realize that even though he might not have been at fault, it appeared otherwise to Eden. Even though Eden exhibited a larger scope of moodiness than most of Thiago's other flings and one-night-stands, at the end of the day, she was the only female he had ever been with who eventually saw reason.

Next stop — the Land of the Fallen Cemetery. If your final destination is the cemetery, please disembark and proceed to Exit A or Exit B. If you wish to transfer to the Runic Territory line, change shuttles here.

Thiago squeezed through the crowds and out the open doorway of the shuttle. He exited the station and stopped at a corner store next to the cemetery. A friendly teenage girl manned the cramped booth in a threadbare coat patterned with illustrated shooting stars. She wore a mask that covered her nose and mouth.

Except for the snow-white scales that covered her body, the girl could almost pass for human. She had black waves of hair that stopped at her shoulders, and wide-set, brown eyes. Born half-Noxx, the orphan had been immediately disowned by society and forced into poverty.

She needed the money she made from the tiny booth to stay afloat. The young girl tended to her shop no matter what the weather conditions were, always displaying a cheerful disposition and a happy-go-lucky attitude that never went stale. Thiago purchased a pair of handmade pillar candles with sparkling moon rocks and blue seashells embedded into the orange wax. He left the girl speechless when he paid for the candles. Thiago was feeling generous and left an enormous tip.

Thiago proceeded through the unmanned gates of the cemetery. The massive graveyard was respectfully silent. Only a handful of visitors wandered through an area that housed over thirty thousand headstones. He headed directly toward a cluster of gravestones situated on the eastern side of the territory.

His solitary footsteps sounded disconcertingly loud against the stone footpath as he passed a sign over an archway. Letters were both missing or hanging on their hinges, but a newcomer could decipher the original words on the sign: **Pacem Village Massacre Resting Ground**.

Except for a few select graves, most of the burial ground lay in miserable conditions. Shriveled plants, incense stubs, and ashes covered abandoned tombstones. Thiago moved off the footpath and made his way through a grid pattern arrangement of graves. As he drew closer to a particular pair of joined headstones near the center of the fourth row, he slowed to a stop.

The twin tombstones of his parents looked freshly polished. The off-white marble shined like it had been made yesterday. Someone had carefully swept old leaves to the side. A gem vase filled with a bouquet of cosmic orchids sat on the patch of grass in front of the headstones. The vibrant petals of the quirky purple and blue orchids sniffled with their persistent illness, adding a dynamic touch to the somber graves.

Thiago knelt on the ground and gazed at the miniature screens embedded on the tombstones above the engraved names and lifespan dates. Six-second scenes displayed in a permanent loop on the screens. The one on the left featured the face of a stern Arkadian man in his mid-fifties. An ill-tailored coat hung loosely over his translucent skin. It looked baked from constant exposure to the sun. The man's trimmed lampshade mustache wiggled like a baby caterpillar above his pursed lips. There were wrinkles around his eyes. It looked as if he were trying not to smile while someone made silly faces in the background.

The screen on the right displayed an attractive human woman in her late forties. The Swedish woman's heavily teased hair ran a little over her defined collarbone. She had the same white-blond locks as her son. Her thick, side-swept bangs bobbed along with her as she laughed soundlessly, tilting her bouncing head back with careless gaiety.

Thiago unpacked his candles and set each one under a headstone. He lit them, using his hand to block out any unwanted drafts. The flames flickered on the wicks as they burned radiantly in contrast to the drearily lit cemetery. Shadows of the night lapped at the sides of Thiago's face. He folded his legs underneath him and sat rigidly still.

In beautiful solitude, the son kept his dead parents company for two hours before he finally left.

Thiago returned to his ship with enough food for two people and a smelly satchel bursting with assorted fish heads for Hercules. He had to juggle everything he was carrying to keep his bag upright in his left hand. At the same time, he balanced the flimsy bags in his right. All the packages were in danger of collapsing under the weight of the stacked seafood and tentacle wonton soup. As he approached the ship, the feeling of relief that should have naturally appeared at the sight of home never arrived. The only emotion he felt was the worry in his heart.

Hercules was going berserk. The creature ran around in erratic circles on the plot of land where Arleda had parked her spaceship. Thiago raced to the animal's side as quickly as possible, sacrificing what he was carrying.

Sloshing soup escaped from overturned lids. Fish heads spun around in his satchel. His pet's mewling whimpers only came to a halt when Thiago arrived at the scene.

"Herc! What's the matter?"

Hercules arched his back and stamped his eight legs on the ground in reply. Thiago dumped the treats from his satchel onto the ground. The creature snapped his pincers, ignoring the mound of fish heads in front of him. Thiago frowned, his brows knitting as he tried to figure out what his pet wanted to communicate.

"You're not upset Arleda's gone, are you? You should be the happiest creature around."

Hercules shook his head angrily. He jerked his head to the left twice. He wanted his master to follow him. Thiago set his satchel and the bags of the remaining soup onto the ground. Scratching at the nape of his neck, he trailed after Hercules inquisitively.

"Where are we going, Herc? We can't mess around now. We need to get back to the ship in case Eden comes home."

Thiago's words faded as he saw something in the scorch marks on the gravel floor which indicated Arleda's recent departure. Hercules lowered his head and nudged a small spherical object in Thiago's direction. He crouched close to the ground to pick it up. A lump formed in his throat as he examined the object in his palms.

He was holding one of the trapped starlight earrings he'd given to Eden the night before the Katakee mission. Rubbing off the dirt caked around the clear glass of the globe, he twirled the post of the earring in his hands. Exhaling deeply, he rose from the ground, brushing off the grains of sand clinging to his pants.

"Let's go, Herc. Eden's not coming back. Arleda's taken her, and we need to bring her home."

CHAPTER 27

"Come on. I need to move faster," Thiago muttered under his breath as he jiggled the ignition lever of the spaceship controls. Warning klaxons blared over the speakers. He squinted at the diminished level of the drained fuel gauge on the corner of the dashboard screen. Shaking his head, he hastily left the cockpit and moved to a storage locker. At the locker, he collected backup jugs of puranium fuel and clamped them under his armpits. He raced back to the cockpit to start refueling.

Hercules slid through the gap of the door just before it sealed shut. He wagged his tongue between his pincers, a puddle of drool pooling underneath him as he watched his master at work.

Thiago lifted a hatch door behind the driver's seat. He unscrewed the caps of the black jugs and tore off the protective seals with his teeth, dispensing the gooey, blue-tinted liquid into the opening of the fuel tank. Hercules moved from side to side behind him, carefully evading the empty jugs of fuel flying in his general direction.

"All right, Herc," Thiago announced. He slammed the hatch door closed and locked the latch with his feet. Swiveling around in his seat to face the dashboard, he started up the ignition. "Hold on, buddy. I'm kicking up the gears, and we're going to be moving quickly."

Hercules nodded, wrapping his bristly legs around the base of the passenger seat. Thiago requested some

information from his shipboard computer, drumming his
fingers on the dashboard as he waited for a tracking page
to load. A complex set of maps complete with grids and
exact coordinates filled the monitor. After inputting a set
of codes on the keypad, the system beeped. A highlighted
route appeared on the map, showing a neon yellow path
leading from the current location of the ship to a general
area that was unfamiliar to the computer.

Thiago's natural inclination for distrusting everyone had
ultimately paid off. Years of a solitary life and never-
ending clashes with polite society may have created a
jaded personality, but it also formed an efficient bounty
hunter. As soon as Arleda had 'stumbled' uninvited into
Thiago's life, he had concealed a tracking device of his
own on her ship.

The ship's wheels rattled against the rugged terrain,
rolling forward on the ground before lifting off into the
air. Thiago steered the vessel at a steep angle as he tried
to accelerate. He angled the spaceship to the left until his
course aligned with the route on the screen.

There was nothing Thiago could do now except wait.
Although his exterior looked like an empty slate, his fists
were clenched impotently around the controls in a death
grip. There was nothing empty about the chaotic anxiety
running rampant through his body. His eyes repeatedly
moved from the windshield to the dashboard screen,
confirming the autopilot was still working.

About two and a half hours later, the triangular symbol
on the craft finally crept toward the flashing dot

indicating Arleda's destination. Rings appeared around the dot, alerting any observers that the journey was almost over. Thiago looked out the windows of the spaceship, trying to find any clue that would help him locate Eden.

The ship hovered over a dark expanse of barren land covered with innumerable craters. Thiago modified the map on his screen to display thermal imagery, which would show him any living beings. To his dismay, nothing but dark blues and greens turned up in the forsaken land underneath him. When the craft began its inevitable descent, Thiago groaned with frustration.

Had the tracker he planted on Arleda's spacecraft been faulty? He didn't see anything here.

Thiago decided to exit his ship to investigate. He transferred the tracking data on his dashboard computer to a portable device in his hands. He exited the cockpit with an excited Hercules hounding him from behind. Thiago packed a spare satchel with flashlights, weapons, rope, rounds of ammunition, and other necessities. He slung the bag over his shoulders before donning a weapon belt strapped with restraints, laser magnums, and a lightweight black-market submachine gun smuggled in from Earth. Fitting his black helmet over his head, he left the ship to begin his search.

As Thiago looked around at the darkness surrounding him, he clicked a button on the side of his helmet visor. The glass whirred to life as his night vision gear activated. He glanced down at the portable tracker in his hands.

According to the computer, he should be close to the location already.

Exploring the site on foot didn't help. He couldn't see anything in the deserted area. Uncertain of what he should be looking for, he started to become frustrated. The mark on his head flashed in anger. Thiago angrily hit the side of the tracker with his fist.

Behind him, Hercules was becoming more agitated. "Not now, Hercules," Thiago called out without looking over his shoulder. "I need to concentrate."

But as Thiago spun around to retrace his steps, he missed his footing entirely. With his complete attention on the computer in his hands, he had neglected his safety. His feet were dangling over the edge of a deep crater. Before Hercules could grab hold of him, Thiago's grip slipped, and he plummeted down the slope of the crater into a pitch-black abyss.

CHAPTER 28

The visor screen on Thiago's helmet intermittently flashed as he flopped back and forth, tumbling down the slope. As a final humiliation, his torso took a beating from a mossy boulder that protruded from the bottom of the crater. Every part of his body hurt when he hit the ground. Rolling like a runaway log, he forced his mouth closed to stop himself from accidentally biting his tongue. Thiago slammed his elbows on the ground. Bits of rubble sprayed around him as he slowed down.

Thiago collected his scattered weaponry and shoved it into his open satchel. He gingerly removed his helmet, looking at the cracks on his visor and examining the damage on its dented and scuffed shell. It was useless now. As he cast it aside, he heard the mournful squeals of Hercules. Moments later, the oversized alien arachnid came sliding down the slope on its back, ending in a slow, spinning stop by his master's feet.

Thiago flattened the crop of hair on top of his buzzed sides. His jumpsuit had holes and patches of missing fabric that had snagged on distended branches on his way down. He winced at the slightest movement of his body.

Something was wrong with his shoulder. Excruciating spasms of pain stabbed at his tender limbs. As veins emerged on his neck and temples, he suppressed an agonized cry as he painfully stretched his arms out in front of him.

Slamming his eyes shut, he clenched his teeth to brace himself. He seized his grotesquely dislocated shoulder and forced it in the opposite direction. A tear fell out of his eye as a sickening crunch sounded and his shoulder snapped back into alignment.

As he held out his shaking arms, he observed his Arkadian genes start to work. The raw, open wounds visible through the shredded fabric of his jumpsuit began to heal. The cuts sealed themselves, leaving darkened traces of scars in their place.

He closed his eyes into focused slits as he analyzed the quarry-like environment. A thick fog of yellow smoke carrying the distinctive stench of sulfur rose from the ground. Steam hissed out from dozens of bubbling acid pits underneath them. On top of the acid pits was a single steel bridge wide enough to fit two tanks side by side. The old surface of the structure was covered with spacecraft scorch marks and tank treads leading to thick, sealed doors in a cavern opening.

Hercules was behind Thiago when the deafening sound of warning sirens shattered the silence. Thiago took a hesitant step backward. His head urgently whipped around in alarm. Hercules gazed back at him with apologetic eyes. His head bowed guiltily, and his legs slowly reversed through a tripwire on the ground.

The pair concealed themselves behind a series of rock formations, pulling their bodies into a tight embrace. Although space was limited, they did what they could to keep their feet stabilized on their patch of land. They shied away from the dangerous acid pits boiling around them. Thiago wrapped his fingers around the rock formation and tried to spy from a distance.

Grating screeches sounded when the heavy doors in the cavern entrance opened. A line of hovering vehicles resembling one-man sleds glided through the doorway, piloted by Noxx soldiers wearing matching uniforms indicating a low rank. Each sled had a mounted laser gun on the curved brush bow on front of the vehicle beds. The mouth of the barrels sparked with striking red bolts. They were ready to kill.

With Hercules' fidgeting head tucked under his armpit, Thiago pulled back his craned neck. He only needed a little space to keep watch. The Noxx maneuvered their sleds around the perimeter in circles. They were determined to find whatever had triggered the tripwire system.

Thiago licked his lips, kneading the creases of his moist palm with his thumb. Thanks to Eden, he had stumbled upon the holy grail of targets for all bounty hunters on the planet. People had searched for this location for decades. Without even meaning to, they had inadvertently found the infamous lair of the feared Noxx.

"All right, buddy. Here goes nothing. Are you ready?" Thiago whispered. He stroked the top of Hercules' head in an attempt to pacify the creature's restlessness. "Lay low for now and wait for my signal before you attack. Do you understand me?"

Hercules nodded enthusiastically in response. He mimed a zipped mouth with a leg held between his pincers. Thiago ripped off his sleeves and tossed them aside, exposing thick muscles on his arms. As beads of sweat raced down the length of his hunched back, he dove into his satchel and rummaged around for a sniper scope. He screwed the scope onto the base of his submachine gun, mounting the weapon against the edge of the flattest rock he could find.

Aligning himself behind the gun, Thiago gazed into the eyepiece. His view crystallized as he adjusted the scope with the parallax ring. The cross of the field slightly moved before he centered it on the closest guard. He was lingering by the foot of the bridge. Thiago slid his finger onto the trigger and tapped the sides of the weapon for good measure with his other hand. Taking one last, soothing breath to calm the thoughts in his head, he gently pulled back the trigger.

An annoying ringing erupted in Thiago's ears as a single bullet shot out from the mouth of his weapon's sizzling barrel. The first of four Noxx enemies was hit directly between the eyes. His vehicle spun off course at once; the front of the sled plunged into the side of the cavern walls before exploding into a flaming fireball.

Before the others could react to their unseen attacker, Thiago had readjusted his scope to aim at his next targets. He kept his finger half-closed on the trigger and gunned down another one. He proved to be resilient when Thiago missed the mark and accidentally hit his stomach. The thug knelt down clutching his midsection until a clean strike to the side of the neck finally rendered him motionless.

The third panicked and tried to flee, abandoning his vehicle. In his flustered state, the Noxx started to run away from danger but accidentally slipped into the acid pit. Unsettling screams of torturous agony made goose bumps spring up on Thiago's arms. The Noxx floundered in the pool until his screams died down and his body vanished.

Thiago tore his eyes away from the gruesome scene, but his distraction had already made him vulnerable to the last Noxx guard. He missed, hitting the arch above the cavern door instead. The goon's sled expertly swerved away from the crumbling debris above him. He slipped away to alert the others.

Thiago swore like a sailor. He tossed his submachine gun aside in favor of the laser magnum on his belt. Swinging his satchel back over his shoulder, he gave Hercules a quick nudge on the leg.

"Let's go."

They darted to the abandoned sled, which was still hovering by the doorway. Thiago grabbed two new puranium orb bombs, pocketing the glass balls. They pulsed with swirling blue contents. The pair raced to the entrance and retraced the steps of the Noxx goon. They ran down a small, dimly lit tunnel that stunk of sewage. Midway through the tunnel, the droning noises of multiple Noxx vehicles intensified. Five enemies in a crisp V-formation appeared at the end of the tunnel, hollering in their native language as they caught sight of the intruders.

Thiago clamped his hands on Hercules' sides, yanking him back as his legs slid underneath him. He spun Hercules around, whisking him off in the opposite direction. The Noxx began firing the mounted laser rifles on their sleighs.

The scrambling duo raced to avoid the red laser bolts. Thiago spotted a recess on the walls of the chamber and took cover, hauling Hercules in with him. Flattening his back against the wall, he pulled out one of the bombs and hurled the explosive sphere into the path of the enemy vehicles.

He closed his eyes, but it didn't help. There was a glaring white flash which temporarily speckled Thiago's vision with glowing blobs of dancing afterimages. A loud explosion followed which sounded like a collision of trains at full speed. They sneaked out of the wall crevice, fanning away the billows of blue smoke and toxic fumes.

Thiago fired his laser magnum, taking out each of the disoriented Noxx sitting dazed in their vehicles before moving past them. Hercules did his share of elimination. He cleared their path by sweeping alien bodies left and right like a rogue demolition worker equipped with a sledgehammer. After the pair fended off about a dozen additional Noxx, they finally arrived at the heart of the lair.

Thiago rapidly assessed the situation in the underground chamber. His eyes lingered on the vessels containing preserved victims. Was Eden in one of them? If she were, she would be stockpiled along the walls like a canned good in an evil supermarket. A complicated series of titanium platforms, winding staircases, and pedestals stood over the frothing lake of acid flowing freely underneath them. Before Thiago could carefully investigate the capsules, a different group of hovering Noxx sailed through the entryway across them.

The bright green bolts that jetted out of Thiago's weapon only managed to scrape the platform of the enemy closest to him before it exhausted its power supply. With the smirking Noxx careening towards him and not enough time to reload, Thiago had to act fast.

He flipped his weapon around and used it to club his assailant on the back of the head. Hercules wrapped his pincers around the Noxx's neck, slashing his arteries before flinging him out of the hijacked sled. The pair clambered into the vehicle. Thiago took the driver's seat as Hercules clung onto the curved back of the chair.

Thiago pulled on a random lever. The sleigh lifted off the ground unsteadily. It tipped from side to side until Thiago became accustomed to the unfamiliar controls. His eyes widened at the sight of Noxx steadily closing the distance between them and beginning to open fire. He steered abruptly to the right, evading the line of laser blasts. He flipping the switches to activate the mounted guns on his sled and his blistered fingertip pulled back a trigger. As he guided the beam of his platform's laser, the smell of singed alien flesh intermingled with the sulfuric air.

Then he heard the sweetest sound in the world.

"Thiago? Oh, thank God – Thiago! I'm up here!"

Thiago looked up, his heart jumping at the sound of Eden's voice. A steel cage hung suspended from the ceiling. It was only accessible by a single staircase that appeared to be at least three stories off the ground. The floor of the cage rocked wildly as Eden excitedly stomped her feet.

He bared his teeth in his wrath, finishing off the rest of the mob moving behind them. He accelerated away from the scene. Hercules gurgled delightedly behind him as they soared up to Eden's height. They hopped off the sled at the top of the staircase. Thiago didn't bother to stop the vehicle, which wasn't large enough to accommodate all three of them. It jerked forward once before plunging into the acid pit underneath them.

"Let's get out of here. I don't know where Malatov and Arleda are, but I think they're coming back at any moment."

"You're okay, Eden. Everything will be fine." He searched in his satchel and pulled out a mechanism resembling a spring clamp. As a puffy-eyed Eden waited in her cage, Thiago fastened the jaws of the tool around the lock. He twisted a knob on the device to activate it.

Within seconds, a powerful laser in the clamp jaws began searing away at the metal.

With Thiago's attention completely absorbed with helping Eden escape, he didn't see what was happening behind him. He didn't notice the wounded Noxx guard moving up the stairs, but Hercules did. As the grunting guard swung a rusty spiked baton over his head, intending to decapitate Thiago, Hercules launched himself at the attacker.

Hercules latched onto the guard, and the grappling pair tumbled over the staircase railing. There was a loud crash and splash into liquid. In moments, acid covered the two bodies.

Thiago and Eden looked at each other in disbelief. For the first time in years, Thiago snapped. The broken man collapsed to his knees. He clutched the sides of his head as their heartbreaking cries filled the vast space of the cavern.

CHAPTER 29

"We have to save Hercules!" Eden's words were drowned out by the roar of an animal-like sobbing.

As the pain of a thousand daggers twisted in his chest, it finally occurred to Thiago that the sounds were coming from his mouth. He was screaming in horror. He felt like a pillow covered his face.

More alarms started to go off in the chamber. They sounded like a symphony of foghorns. Thiago stopped looking at the ground, numbly observing the groups of Noxx pouring through all four entrances around them. He only broke out of his haze when he noticed the sneering faces of Malatov and Arleda among the mob of white scaly bastards. An adrenaline rush fueled with hatred and bloodlust drove him to his feet.

"Thiago! Get me out of here. They're coming!"

Thiago broke off the lock hanging from the cage and entered the tiny quarters. He refilled his laser magnum with clips of ammunition and fired at the hinges of the shackles. Eden's outstretched limbs fell from over her head. She yelped in pain as she slammed to the ground. Thiago snapped off Eden's cuffs, giving her a powerful hug before set her free.

"Don't leave me again. I can't protect you if you run away. Can you move?"

"Yes. I'm sore as hell, but the feeling's slowly coming back to my legs."

"Here," said Thiago. He handed her a spare laser pistol from his satchel and the last orb bomb he'd collected from the abandoned sled. He took a moment to instruct her on how to operate the weapon.

He motioned to a switch on the side of the barrel and said, "The blue light's for stun, and the green light's for kill. Be careful with the orb. It's fragile, explosive, and dangerous."

"Okay, I got it," said Eden. The magnum shook in her hands as she slipped it into her belt strap. Peering over Thiago's shoulder, she gasped. Her eyes went round with terror at the Noxx guards gathering at the foot of the staircase. "Can we evade these guys?"

"We'll get them. Be careful." Thiago lifted Eden off the ground and started toward the open cage door.

"Thiago, wait." Eden pulled him down for a kiss. "Be careful, please."

Thiago paused. He tried to press his lips tightly together, but he couldn't help smiling.

"I will. Now let's get these bastards."

Eden threw away her useless heels. Her legs felt like lead underneath her as she ran after Thiago and she looked a filthy, bedraggled mess. Vast areas of her soiled halter jumpsuit were missing sequins. Inflamed alien bug bites peppered her dingy bare arms. The nest of coppery curls that ran past her shoulders had fluffed up from the humidity; it was untamable. Fortunately for Eden, there was no mirror, and discomfort was the last thing on her mind.

Thiago's aim seemed to improve in his trance-like rage. His barrel zeroed in on each of the Noxx running up the staircase, efficiently eliminating each target. Without looking behind him, he grabbed hold of two clips and put them into the chamber of his gun, reloading with mechanical efficiency.

Thiago and Eden started shooting in turns. One began firing while the other reloaded. Fallen guards toppled backward, creating an inescapable domino effect upon the soldiers behind them. As Thiago exterminated the last few attempting to crawl over their comrades' bodies, Eden sidled past them and down the stairs, knocking a few wounded guards over the railing along the way.

She was on a mission.

Eden made a beeline for Arleda. The beaming Arkadian woman stood with her spread legs locked and her arms folded across her chest. Her face looked primped for a red carpet, and her glossy pink hair stayed in place with two bejeweled hairpins. Even in the face of chaos, Arleda was as glamorous as ever.

Eden snorted, flicking away the sweat dangling off her nostrils. There was nothing more she wanted at that moment than to wipe the smug look off Arleda's face. The green bulb flashed on the nose of her pistol. But as Eden raised her weapon, Arleda lunged forward with a high kick and knocked the gun out of Eden's hands.

The weapon bounced on the ground and slid out of reach. Their eyes met for a split second before they both dove for the laser pistol. Eden knew her human strength wouldn't be enough to win against Arleda's Arkadian genes, so she had to resort to rough playground tactics. Eden sprang on top of Arleda and straddled her. She weaved her hands into the threads of Arleda's hair, immobilizing her bun as she pulled and twisted. Arleda shrieked. Tears fell from her eyes as Eden's fists tore off clumps of her hair.

Arleda shook her off, panting heavily. In her discombobulated state, she made the mistake of turning her back on Eden for one brief moment. Eden jumped at the chance, reaching for the orb bomb tucked away in her bra. She bit down on her lip and twisted the sphere to activate it. As Arleda turned back around, Eden stuffed the orb into her mouth. Finally, she gave Arleda a push.

Arleda's eyes bulged in astonishment. Her arms and legs flailed as she fell towards the acid pit behind her. Her cheeks ballooned and turned a ghostly blue before the orb detonated in her mouth. Body parts and jewelry rained into the murky yellow sea from above.

Gagging from the putrid stench, Eden whirled around, looking for Thiago. He was fighting with Maltov in a different struggle beyond the bodies of Noxx guards strewn across the floor. Eden watched as Thiago rolled on top of Malatov, jamming the barrel of his magnum between the Noxx's lips.

"Don't kill him!" Eden called out.

"Not now, Eden," Thiago hissed through clenched teeth. The marking on his forehead glowed a fiery red. "What about my parents?"

"He doesn't deserve a quick death," wheezed Eden as she ran up from behind him. She grabbed hold of his shoulder, squeezing. "Let the asshole rot in prison. We also need his face intact to collect the bounty."

Thiago struggled with himself as his shaking finger hovered over the trigger. He glared at Malatov's steely, unfeeling eyes blinking back at him.

His rational mind prevailed in a moment, and he let his body relax. He removed the weapon from Malatov's mouth.

"It's over now."

Thiago put restraints onto Malatov's wrists. He allowed himself one luxury, however. Thiago blew a glob of spit into Malatov's leering face before Thiago and Eden turned around, leaving the Noxx kingpin's empty threats behind them.

CHAPTER 30

THREE MONTHS LATER

"Why don't you set the ship to autopilot so you can enjoy a glass of bubbly?"

Thiago looked over his shoulder and smiled. Eden had noticed he was happier recently, and not a morose stick-in-the-mud like when she first met him. She entered the cockpit, carrying an expensive bottle of vintage Pasquin ale in one hand and a fancy goblet engraved with ancient Arkadian hieroglyphics in the other. She looked stunning in an emerald green dress which accented her eyes. The asymmetrical neckline showed off a hint of her delicate collarbone.

He let the computer take over the ship and swiveled around in his chair to face Eden. She uncorked the bottle and poured a golden liquid into the glass, handing it to him. Sensing something was wrong, Eden tipped her head to the side and frowned.

"Is something the matter, honey?" she whispered. She snuggled up to him, gently massaging the hard knots permanently lodged in his neck and shoulders.

"It's nothing. I'm just a little tired of tossing and turning on the new mattress we bought last week."

"Me too. It's going to take a few more nighttime activities before we break it in," Eden said with a grin. She sighed and traced her finger along the buzzed sides of Thiago's head. "If a new mattress is our biggest problem, we've got a good thing going here. Malatov's going to prison as we speak. You're practically a celebrity now, and the payout for his capture was more than we had ever imagined. My family on Earth is living happy and debt-free. I'd say our life is divine right now, don't you think?"

"I suppose so," Thiago replied. He chugged back the rest of his ale and placed the empty goblet on the dashboard.

Eden took the passenger's seat and tapped her toes nervously against the leg of her chair. She wanted to say something to Thiago, but she wasn't sure how to open the topic of conversation.

"You know what this place needs? A little music."

Pulling up the radio on his dashboard screen, she selected a random station and started the music. A faint tune drifted through the speakers before the system sparked and died out. Eden pressed some random buttons, but they had no effect. Thiago bent forward in his seat and removed the cone of the exterior speaker.

"Well, this is a surprise."

The cone dropped between Thiago's feet. Eden clapped a hand over her mouth. Two baby alien arachnids the size of newborn puppies crawled out of the speaker opening. They each scooped one onto their lap. Thiago and Eden's heads hit each other as they peered into the radio opening. Two large broken eggs with purple polka-dots on their shells were nested deep inside the ship, incubated by the warmth.

"Hercules was a girl!" Eden said, gently crooning as she tickled the giggling creature in her lap.

"I suppose she was," said Thiago, his cheeks flushing with rosy affection at the baby animal burrowed in his lap. He glanced up at Eden. "This is amazing. I'm glad Hercules will live on, in a way, through her children. Why don't you take this one, too? These babies call for a proper celebration. You can't have any of the Pasquin ale, but I think there's some honeyberry champagne in the refrigerator that's safe for humans."

"No. I can't."

"Why not?"

Eden lowered her eyes meaningfully, rubbing one hand on her stomach. "Hercules wasn't the only mother on board."

Thiago smiled as Eden took his cold, clammy hand and warmed wrapped it between her palms. The pair leaned in close together. The tips of their noses touched as their lips locked in a long, passionate kiss. When they finally broke apart, their eyes stared out into the distance.

A new adventure awaited them beyond the fluffy formations of pink clouds on the horizon.

If you enjoyed this book, please review it on Amazon. Your review helps me succeed as an author.

To stay up-to-date on my latest releases, sign up for my newsletter at:

http://lisalace.com/newsletter/

OTHER BOOKS BY LISA LACE

WATER WORLD WARRIOR: A TerraMates Novel

Why would I want to be married to an alien?

I should not have applied to TerraMates! The idea was crazy. I'm a young woman, in the prime of my life.

But I was desperate.

When I landed on another world, his appearance intrigued me. He dripped sexuality and moved like an animal. We have three days together before he sets sail without me. Am I going to escape or submit to my desires?

TAKEN: A TerraMates Novel

What happens when TerraMates runs out of applicants?

There's never a shortage of wealthy alien bachelors looking for the thrill of mating with a human. They want our women.

But despite the promise of riches, sometimes the pool of available brides runs dry.

How does TerraMates find more girls, and where do they go? When Lyzette gets taken off the street, she finds out.

Water World Confidential: A TerraMates Novel

He needed a wife. I wanted an alien lover.

The first time I saw Jori, I hated everything about him. He didn't care about anything except himself. On the other hand, his body was spectacular, and his muscles were firm. I couldn't stop thinking about him.

When TerraMates gave me the chance to marry Jori, I took it. I knew I needed the money. What I didn't know was that Jori's exterior was a facade, and he had kept secrets from everyone his entire life.

Alpha's Enslaved Bride: A TerraMates Novel

Knowing the future isn't a blessing. It's a curse. Especially when you've seen your death.

I'm going to die in the arms of someone I have never seen before. He's a person I will love, but I don't know anything about him.

When TerraMates matched me with Airik, I couldn't believe it. This sexy alien could see the future, just like me. I wasn't alone anymore. I quickly found out he knows nothing about Earth or humans. I married him, but will I be safe with him?

I didn't foresee I would want to feel his hands on my body.

I've never been able to change the future before. For us to survive, I need to.

CAPTURED BY THE ALIEN KING

When I saw my chance to get off Earth, I took it. I knew I needed to escape.

I didn't know I'd be claimed by an alien monarch in the middle of his mating season! Now we're on the run together, facing terrorists and natural disasters.

I'm still trying to figure out my feelings for this sexy guy. He is totally into me, but he has some unique ideas about alien romance...

www.ingramcontent.com/pod-product-compliance
Lightning Source LLC
Chambersburg PA
CBHW020603180626
46810CB00007B/2628